CRATCHIT

"A CHRISTMAS CAROL" CONTINUES

R.M. BOUKNIGHT

ISBN: 979-8-9998307-1-5
First edition
Printed in the United States of America

Published by Hollybridge Books

Author's Note:

This book would not have been possible without the genius of Charles Dickens, whose timeless tale *A Christmas Carol* continues to entertain and enlighten.

Content Note:

This story touches on moments of emotional struggle and unspoken pain, approached with compassion and sensitivity. These elements are part of a larger journey filled with resilience, humor, healing, and hope.

To my wife,
who keeps Christmas in her heart
all year round.

And to my family,
who has made me a better man—
not in one miraculous night,
but over one gratifying lifetime.

CRATCHIT
"A CHRISTMAS CAROL" CONTINUES

CONTENTS

PROLOGUE

The Night of Christmas Eve

The doors flew open as if by some unseen force, and Bob Cratchit stumbled into the snow-swept night, eyes burning, heart pounding.

The laughter. He had to escape the cruel chorus of mocking laughter echoing in his ears.

The bell in the clock tower was striking the midnight hour, loud and unrelenting.

Cratchit raced down the steps into the roadway, aimless and alone. Wind clawed at his coat as he ran through the streets of London, past shuttered shops and alleys choked with snowdrifts.

He stopped to catch his breath, clamping his hands over his ears. But it was no use. The clanging and laughter were not diminishing. They were growing louder.

Another sound broke through. At first, Cratchit thought it was thunder.

Then he realized, it was hooves. Heavy and fast. Closing in.

He began running again, ignoring the burning in his lungs, shoes slipping on the slick cobblestones. Dazed and disoriented, he lurched into a crossroads—then froze.

Four monstrous black horses surged out of the darkness, bearing down on him. Their eyes glowed red, their manes lashed in the wind. Steam burst from their nostrils, and sparks flew as their hooves struck the stones.

There was no time to save himself. Cratchit raised his hands and braced for impact.

Stave One

The Morning of Christmas Eve

I've related to you the story of Ebenezer Scrooge, a hard-hearted soul whose life was changed in a single night. But that wasn't the end of my story. No, you've heard only half the tale. For even men of true heart can be blinded by temptation, and risk losing everything in this world they hold dear.

Such was the fate of Scrooge's clerk, Bob Cratchit.

Though morning sunlight filtered through his bedroom windows, Cratchit remained fast asleep, sprawled in an armchair. Like bellows stoking a furnace, his snores rumbled through the chamber.

It had been another night of revelry. He was still dressed in last evening's clothes. His frock coat was now rumpled, his cravat askew, his waistcoat straining at the buttons. An empty gin bottle dangled from one hand while the other cradled a glass with a splash remaining.

Chester, a small terrier of boundless energy and little sense, was lapping up the last of Cratchit's drink.

The room was still. The door closed. The windows shut tight.

And yet, the drapes stirred—softly, suddenly—as if brushed by a draft.

The muslin bed canopy rustled faintly. The flame in the lamp quivered.

From the floorboards near the hearth came a slow, groaning creak. Chester raised his head at the sound, ears twitching.

And then—a shadow, long and formless. It crept from the hearth like spilled ink, gliding slowly across the floor, coming to rest above Cratchit, where it lingered, silent and still.

Cratchit snorted and shifted in his sleep. The gin bottle slipped from his grasp and struck the floor with a sharp clatter, startling him awake.

"Wh—What? Who's there?" he muttered, disoriented. His eyes swept the room before glancing down to see he still held a tumbler with a sip of gin. He considered it for a moment, gave a shrug, and drained the glass.

"Hair of the dog," he said to Chester. The little terrier yapped once in reply.

Downstairs, the kitchen of the Cratchit home bustled with a warmth that stood in sharp contrast to the morning's chill. The air was thick with the scent of cinnamon, though a faint note of scorched oats lingered.

Belinda Cratchit, now a young woman of twenty-four, moved with quiet precision at the stove. Her golden curls were pinned back from a face flushed rosy by the fire. She stirred a pot of porridge, her fingers still sore from hemming gowns. Her days were spent at the dressmaker's shop, so the housework was often not completed until late at night. With her mother gone, the running of the household had fallen squarely upon her shoulders.

She exchanged morning greetings with her father as he entered the kitchen, now dressed for work. Cratchit collapsed into a chair with the grace of a falling sack. Planting his elbows on the table, he rubbed his temples, trying to erase the ache in his head.

"Did you sleep well?" Belinda asked, placing a bowl of porridge before him.

"Not a wink," he sighed.

Chester leapt onto the opposite chair and rested his chin on the table, commiserating with his master.

"Will you be attending Christmas services with us tomorrow?" Belinda asked brightly.

He waved the suggestion away. "I'll be there—in spirit."

"That's hardly the same as being there in person."

"If you recall," he said, "the last time I was in church, it ended rather poorly for me, Belinda."

He put a spoonful of porridge in his mouth. His face instantly contorted into a grimace.

"How do you like it?" she asked, her back turned as she stirred the pot.

"It's—delightful," he lied, cheeks bulging. He quietly spat the porridge back into his bowl.

"It's a new recipe. From France," she added cheerfully.

"Yet another offense committed by the French," he whispered to Chester, secretly scraping the mush into the dog's dish. Chester sniffed it, whimpered, and retreated.

Belinda turned and caught sight of the empty bowl. "Well now, you *did* like my porridge! Another bowl?"

"Good heavens, no! I couldn't eat another bite," Cratchit said hastily, rising. As he made for the parlor door, Belinda stepped into his path and held out a neatly wrapped box. "It's a Christmas present. From Mother."

Cratchit stared at it, then reluctantly peeled back the paper and opened the box. Inside was a long red scarf, hand-stitched. She wrapped the scarf gently around his neck.

"She still loves you, you know," Belinda said softly.

"Then why is she not here?" he asked.

Belinda placed her hand lightly on the scarf. "It would be so nice if we were all together for the holidays."

"Yes," he said flatly. "It would be a Christmas miracle."

A concerned expression suddenly came over his face, and he began patting his coat pockets. Belinda hesitated, then reached into her apron and produced a silver flask, offering it to him.

"I filled it for you," she said.

Cratchit smiled and took the flask, sliding it safely into his pocket.

"What would I do without you, my dear?"

He turned and walked briskly into the parlor. Belinda followed, the hem of her dress whispering across the floor.

"I'll see you tonight at the Christmas party?" she asked.

"Yes, of course," he replied.

"Promise me the first dance?"

"If you wish," he said.

"Will Mother be there?"

"You'll have to ask *her* that," he replied curtly.

"Have you been—"

"Enough questions, Belinda!" he snapped, his words striking with the force of a slap.

She abruptly stopped walking. Her eyes dropped, shoulders folding inward.

Cratchit turned and saw his daughter looking at the floor. The sternness faded from his face. He sighed, stepped back to her, and gently lifted her chin.

"You'll have the first dance tonight," he said quietly. "I promise you."

Trying to coax a smile from her, he began to hum. Taking her hand, he cradled her waist and swayed with her. She resisted at first, but he nudged her gently, easing her into a waltz that grew livelier as his singing grew bolder.

They danced in small circles around the parlor, her father's earlier rebuke fading behind a reluctant smile. He ended the dance with a playful flourish, spinning her out, then snatching his stovepipe hat and cane before stepping briskly out the door.

Belinda stood motionless as the latch clicked behind him. Slowly, her smile faded. She crossed her arms and rubbed her forearms in slow, absent strokes.

Slightly winded from the dance, Cratchit leaned on his cane for a moment to catch his breath. He realized that he was no longer the man he used to be. Over the years, his eyes had grown a bit weaker, his joints a bit stiffer. He had imagined himself growing older gracefully, but grace seemed to be slipping further away. Each new ache and pain reminded him of the race he was running against Time. He knew it was a race he would eventually lose—

though he could do without Time snickering at every stumble.

Cratchit's house stood at the end of a quiet crescent, a terraced home three stories in height. Its bay window bowed slightly outward as if giving a courteous nod to the street. Iron railings bordered a neat garden patch hardly larger than a bath sheet (but how proud Cratchit was of that garden patch!)

This peaceful corner of London was far removed from the soot-choked alleys of Camden Town, where he once lived—eight people in a four-roomed house! Cratchit descended his steps with the quiet satisfaction of a man who had climbed the ladder—just high enough to glimpse the comforts enjoyed by those on the other side of the wall.

At the corner where the crescent curved into the main road, he paused. A group of boys had claimed a frozen strip of pavement. With coats flapping and boots skimming, they took turns dashing at full pelt, launching themselves into a glorious slide.

Cratchit observed the boys' activity with a smile, recalling a Christmas Eve when he went down a slide on Cornhill. What was it—thirteen years ago? Twenty times he'd gone down, laughing like a fool. He wouldn't dare now, of course. What would people think?

He turned his collar up against the cold and made his way toward the town square. Snow dusted the rooftops and softened the cobblestones. The gas lamps, still aglow from the night before, shimmered faintly on frost-laced panes. Iron-wheeled carts trundled past, laden with mistletoe, holly, and wreaths of pine.

Two pretty young women approached with matching white fur hats and muffs, cheeks flushed from the cold. "Morning, ladies," he greeted them, bowing and tipping his hat. The women giggled as they passed. Cratchit turned his head to admire their swaying bustles as they sashayed away.

Pressing on toward his place of business, Cratchit casually glanced into the windows of shops dressed in festive fir garlands and red ribbons, nestled between cold, gray office buildings that displayed not one hint of the holiday season inside or out. Through one fogged pane, he caught sight of a young worker hunched over a desk, cupping his hands above a stub of candle for warmth. A strange pang of recognition stirred in Cratchit's chest. He had been that man once, a clerk bent beneath the chill draft of the counting house, scratching ink across ledgers for barely enough coin to keep meat in the pot.

Turning a corner, Cratchit entered the town square, alive with morning life. Shopkeepers opened their doors with ritual precision, children darted between stalls in pursuit of mischief, carolers filled the air with song on the corner. The bells of nearby churches pealed the hour in cheerful succession, competing with the cry from hawkers selling their wares with enthusiasm undiminished by the cold.

At the square's center rose a statue, larger than life, carved of pale marble. A familiar face looked down kindly upon all passersby, a gentle smile carved into chiseled stone. The base was covered in candles, coins, and flowers that people had left in remembrance. Etched into the pedestal was the name: EBENEZER SCROOGE.

Cratchit stopped in front of the statue. An elderly woman approached, brushing his coat sleeve as she passed by. She gently placed a handful of peonies among the other tributes, genuflecting in front of the statue before stepping back and standing beside Cratchit with tear-filled eyes.

"God bless you, Mr. Scrooge," she said, her voice cracking. "You was a saint, you was."

She dabbed her eyes with a torn lace kerchief, offering no other words, only one last quivering breath before drifting away into the crowd.

Cratchit watched her go, slowly shaking his head. He turned to face the statue, raised an eyebrow, and muttered: "In your own words, Ebenezer—humbug!"

He couldn't bear the way the man still rose above him.

A familiar voice drifted from a nearby stall, strong and thick with the tang of the Thames. Cratchit turned and walked over to the fish stand. "What looks good today?" he asked.

The fishmonger leaned over the counter, his broad, oil-stained hands gripping the edge of the stall. He wore a striped apron smeared with scales and salt, a cap pushed askew atop his head.

"In the second race at Ascot," he said in a low, Cockney drawl, "I like the three-to-one—Bonny Lee."

Cratchit gave him a skeptical look. "Are you confident of this?"

"I talked to the horse meself this morning," the fishmonger replied with a wink, releasing a puff of brine-scented breath.

Cratchit snorted. "The last time you conversed with a horse, I lost a week's wages."

The man gave a philosophical shrug. “He lied to me, that one did. He’s a bottle of glue now, the old sod.”

Suppressing a smirk, Cratchit reached into his coat pocket and handed over a bag of coins. “Six quid on Bonny Lee to win.”

With all the solemnity of a banker sealing a bond, the fishmonger pocketed the coins, wrapped a glistening cod in yesterday’s newspaper, and passed it across the counter. Cratchit tucked the parcel beneath his arm and resumed his walk, while the fishmonger returned to hawking with renewed vigor.

The offices of Cratchit and Sons stood along a respectable street, its grandeur a jarring contrast to the neighborhood’s understated charm. An ornate copper door, polished daily by a boy in livery, gleamed at the entrance.

In front of the building, a soldier in a battle-worn uniform sat beside a street grate, drawing what warmth he could from the steam rising below. His eyes were downcast, his face hollowed by hardship. He held a cap loosely in his lap, soliciting alms in silence.

Cratchit was about to pass by the soldier. But then, thinking better of it, he stepped over to the destitute man.

“Frightful weather,” Cratchit murmured as he drew his coat tighter around himself. The soldier did not answer.

Cratchit looked about, tucking the wrapped cod under the opposite arm. He reached into his coat pocket and produced a gold coin.

“You’ll forgive me,” he said softly as he leaned down and placed the coin in the soldier’s hat, “but might I ask you to sit—*elsewhere*?”

The soldier slowly looked up. As their eyes met, Cratchit smiled. He wondered if he was the only person who'd shown compassion to the poor soul all morning. He knew he'd been overly generous, but after all, it was Christmas Eve.

The solder picked the sovereign from the cap and looked it over, turning it side to side. Then, meeting Cratchit's gaze again, he extended his arm—and dropped it into the street grate without a word.

Cratchit pressed his lips together and gave a sharp snort, taken aback that his gesture of goodwill would be met with ingratitude. Flustered, he turned and entered the building.

Clerks were already busy at work, hunched over ledgers, pens scratching in rhythmic tandem; a junior solicitor conferred with the chief accountant; two errand boys hovered by the delivery alcove.

Mary Fielding, all of twenty years and possessed of an intellect far sharper than many twice her age, searched through the filing drawer behind her desk. There was something in her manner—composed, assured—that unsettled those who dismissed her at a glance. Her features struck a harmony of contrasts: a determined mouth beneath watchful eyes, dark chestnut hair pinned back, though a defiant curl had escaped to graze her cheek. As she leaned forward, a fine gold chain slipped into view, an heirloom from her grandmother in Kraków.

Pausing her search, Mary sniffed the air, picking up an unusual scent of brine. Slowly swiveling in her seat, she met the bug-eyed stare of a cod wrapped in newsprint on her desk.

Inside his office, Cratchit squeezed a few drops of laudanum from a dropper into his mouth. He capped the small blue bottle just as Mary entered with an armful of papers.

"Opium so early in the morning, Mr. Cratchit?" she asked, with a mix of concern and accusation.

"You know very well it's for my rheumatism, Mary," Cratchit responded, not quite meeting her eye.

Mary placed papers on the desk with quiet efficiency. "These require your signature."

As she handed him a pen, her other hand quietly reached for the bottle and secretly slipped it into her apron pocket without a word. (Later, she would empty the bottle and refill it with plain water. It had become a common routine, and Mr. Cratchit never seemed to notice the difference.)

He gave an exaggerated sigh at the stack of papers, perched a pair of reading glasses on the end of his nose, and began signing. He glanced up at Mary briefly before saying with deliberate casualness, "You know, Tim returns from Ireland today."

"Yes, I know," she said quickly—too quickly, she realized—a flush rising to her cheeks. Cratchit smiled in amusement, knowing she did not embarrass easily.

"Why, Mary," he said, "you're even *more beautiful* when you're blushing."

Cratchit fancied himself a gentleman of generous observation, one who unabashedly complimented beauty wherever it chanced to bloom. Was it not, after all, a kindness to brighten a young woman's day with a well-placed remark?

Mary rapped him smartly across the knuckles with his own desk ruler. "Ow!" he exclaimed, wincing and shaking his hand in the air.

"Such compliments should be reserved solely for your wife, Mr. Cratchit," she said, correcting him with the cheerful firmness of a governess who expected no backtalk. "That being said—thank you."

Peter Cratchit approached the entrance of Cratchit and Sons with the bearing of a man accustomed to responsibility. He was clad in a dark wool coat trimmed at the lapels, and a collar that framed his sharp features. His hair, thick and flaxen, bore a touch of gray at the temples—not from age (for he was only twenty-seven), but from weightier causes. He carried himself like one who watched over others, even while battling demons of his own.

Peter paused when he noticed the soldier still sitting outside the building. Both their breaths curled upward in the morning air.

"What was your regiment, soldier?" he asked.

The man blew into his cupped hands and said nothing.

"It's freezing. Come inside and warm yourself." Then, as much to himself as to the soldier he murmured, "Of course, I can't guarantee that the heat will be working."

Still no response from the man.

"We're having a Christmas party this evening," Peter went on. "I'd be honored if you could attend."

"You'd be honored?" the soldier finally replied, revealing a hint of a Scottish accent. He nodded his head toward the building. "I don't belong in there."

"No," Peter replied, quiet but firm, "you don't belong out *here*."

The soldier said nothing, just stared at the cobblestones.

Cratchit read aloud under his breath as he scanned the last sheet of paper, a list of items for that night's celebration. Suddenly, he raised his voice in alarm. "Mary! *Two shillings* for raspberry tarts?"

She looked at the sheet. "Too much?"

"Not enough!" he replied. "What if we were to run out?"

She began collecting the papers. "Should that happen, Mr. Cratchit, I'll walk to the baker's myself and secure more tarts—so that Christmas might be saved."

She turned to go, but then paused. "Do you think Tim will make it back in time for the party?"

"Yes, I've no doubt my brother will make his *usual* grand entrance," Peter said dryly as he strode into the office. He greeted Mary with a courteous nod, which she returned before making her way to the door.

"Father, it's imperative I speak with you about company finances," said Peter.

"Another time, Peter," Cratchit responded.

Mary turned as she reached the doorway. "Oh, Mr. Cratchit—is that *your* fish on my desk?"

"It's *yours*," he said with a magnanimous wave of his arms. "Merry Christmas."

Mary blinked, and managed to force a smile. Then, catching himself, Cratchit added, "Or as your people would say—*shalom*."

Mary blinked again, not knowing how to respond. "Shalom," she said, before turning and leaving the room.

Cratchit began opening letters with a finely wrought sterling paperknife, a gift from his wife. Longer and sturdier than most, its handle was engraved with his initials.

"What news from the markets today, Peter?"

Peter took down a thick volume from the bookcase. "The money markets are strong."

Cratchit nodded. "Splendid."

Peter dropped the heavy book on the desk. "This firm, however, is overextended and unprepared for Revaluation Day."

"Nonsense," Cratchit said dismissively.

Peter opened the book in front of his father. "The company continues to borrow heavily from those scoundrels who claim to be your friends."

"At excellent rates, I might add," Cratchit replied.

"But that changes *tomorrow*," Peter said, raising his voice.

Cratchit rose from his chair, tossing the paperknife and letters on his desk. "I've been assured that the rate increases will be minimal."

"*You've been assured*," Peter laughed. "They're gutting this firm, and you're handing them the knife. Mr. Scrooge would never have allowed it."

"Ebenezer Scrooge is quite dead and therefore has nothing to say about it!" Cratchit shouted, slamming the heavy book shut. "Why must you question my judgment?"

"And why must you *ignore* mine?"

"The loans we received are from men of their word," Cratchit countered, walking to Peter.

"They are liars and thieves preying on a vain old man too proud to admit he's been duped!"

Cratchit's open hand flew before he could stop it, striking Peter's face with a sharp crack. Peter didn't flinch. He met his father's eyes with quiet force.

"You never hit any one of us before, Father," he said. "I suggest you not begin the practice now."

Their attention was drawn by a polite clearing of the throat. Randall Yates stood at the door with the quiet confidence of a clerk intent on rising through the ranks. His dark eyes and bronze complexion hinted at his ancestry, but his manner and speech were perfectly British.

"Mr. Cratchit—" he said, nodding toward four gentlemen waiting beyond the glass.

Peter glanced at the group. "Speak of the devils," he murmured.

Cratchit waved them in with cheerful familiarity, and Randall opened the door wide. Three of the men entered first, each dressed in the solemn finery of London's mercantile elite—dark wool frock coats tailored close to the frame, crisp cravats tied with deliberate precision. Cratchit seized each man's hand eagerly, saying their name in turn: "Mr. Hawkins. Mr. Quill. Mr. Ramsey—" As he shook hands, his eyes drifted—as they always did—to the identical gold rings worn by each man, engraved with the image of a silver chalice.

The final man entered with quiet composure, his presence commanding, like a gentleman unhurried by time.

"—and Mr. Thatch!" Cratchit said, eyes lighting up.

Thatch's black frock coat was impeccably tailored, the cloth fine enough to whisper of Savile Row. A silver watch chain traced a perfect arc across his waistcoat. His hair, dark with streaks of silver, was neatly combed back from a high brow, revealing features marked by intelligence and reserve. His eyes, pale and piercing, seemed always to be calculating. When he smiled, it was with the faintest upturn of the mouth. His friends found it charming; his enemies found it chilling.

"Bob!" Thatch greeted him. "Merry Christmas, old fellow!"

Ramsey held up an antique pewter hourglass, with a red bow on top.

"A gift," said Thatch, "to remind you that we always have *time* for our clients."

"Lovely!" Cratchit remarked appreciatively, placing the hourglass on his desk. "To what do I owe the honor of this visit?"

Hawkins, lean and always squinting, stepped forward. "We were planning a night of holiday revelry—"

"—and hoping that you would be free to join us this evening," Ramsey finished. His prodigious facial hair was impeccably coiffed, making him look more owl than man.

"Have you ever known me to refuse?" Cratchit asked.

"Never!" Quill answered, laughing, his ample belly shaking like St. Nick's.

"Then tonight will be no exception!" Cratchit declared. The group responded with good-natured laughter. Peter, standing stiffly by, cast his father a withering glance.

"*After* our company Christmas party is over, of course," Cratchit added.

Thatch's smile flickered. His gaze drifted over to Peter. "Bob, might we have a word with you—in private?"

Peter's expression soured. Without a word, he turned and stepped out. Thatch closed the door behind him with a slow, deliberate click.

Peter joined Randall and Mr. Hobbs out on the main floor. Hobbs, the firm's eldest accountant, was hunched beside a pile of ledgers. With his constant muttering, he was a one-man rumor mill.

"Look at 'em," Hobbs said, nodding toward the office. "Like a flock o' ruddy vultures pickin' your father's bones dry. They always go after the weak ones."

Peter raised an eyebrow. "*Weak* ones?"

"You know," Hobbs said as he mimed tipping back a bottle. "You ought to be runnin' the company, Peter. Not your father."

Randall glanced over with interest, though he quickly looked away when Peter caught his eye.

"He'll have us all in the poor house soon, he will," Hobbs mumbled.

"Attend to your work, Mr. Hobbs," Peter said sharply.

Hobbs grumbled and turned back to his figures just as Cratchit's office door opened. The four men emerged, laughing, Cratchit following behind them. "Peter, would you be kind enough to show these good gentlemen the door?"

"See them out? With pleasure," Peter replied, and began leading the four businessmen to the front.

As they passed Mary's desk, Thatch turned his head toward her just as she looked up. She gave him a reserved, polite nod. He did not return it, only fixed her with a cool, unreadable stare before turning his head back to Peter.

"Your father has a head for business," Thatch said. "He could teach you a thing or two, Master Cratchit."

"*Mister* Cratchit," Peter corrected him. "Between school, my father, and Mr. Scrooge, I've had an excellent education in business. I know how to invest money wisely—" He stopped at the front door. "—and I know a *bad* investment when I see one."

Thatch arched a brow. "Do I detect a note of distrust, Mr. Cratchit?"

Peter smiled coolly. "More than a note. An entire symphony, Mr. Thatch."

Thatch put his hand on Peter's shoulder cordially and leaned in closer. "We have only your father's best interests in mind, son," he said softly.

"I believe I know what you have in mind for my father," Peter said, opening the door. "Good day, gentlemen."

The three men filed out of the building, but Thatch didn't move. He continued to smile, carefully studying Peter's face before slowly tipping his hat, and joining the other businessmen.

Closing the door as if he had just expelled beetles from a breadbox, Peter turned and glanced about the main floor. He sighed. The building was a daily reminder of what he considered to be his father's yearning for status.

Conceived entirely by Bob Cratchit himself, the space was lofty, well-appointed—and thoroughly overstated. The kind of grandeur that strained to impress.

The expansion had begun as an ambitious vision three years prior. Cratchit had ordered the old ceiling demolished to create a soaring, double-height atrium. Floor-to-ceiling bookshelves lined the walls, punctuated by marble busts of poets and philosophers. Above the row of private offices with leaded glass panels framed in polished walnut paneling, an ornate staircase led to an open second-floor gallery. From the vaulted ceiling hung two expensive Belgian chandeliers; delicate, refined, and utterly lost in the vastness above.

The room was heated by one of Cratchit's proudest indulgences: a modern hot-water radiator system. It worked roughly half of the time.

At the center of the room stood a large circular "wishing" fountain made of marble. Meant to be a centerpiece, it was mostly an obstruction. The staff had tossed a few coins into the basin, perhaps wishing it would go away.

Along one wall, Cratchit had arranged "a place for quiet conversation," where no conversations ever took place. Two stiff-backed chairs flanked a grand marble fireplace that was just a façade, built against a wall with no chimney.

In short, it was a building desperately trying to become something it was not.

As Peter walked to his office, a worker high above him balanced precariously on a rail-mounted ladder, his arms overloaded with books. Pulling volumes from the top shelf, he let one heavy tome slip from his grasp.

The book struck the wooden floor with a deafening crack. Peter spun toward the sound, eyes wide, breath shallow.

He was no longer in an office. He was on a battlefield, the air thick with smoke and the stench of iron. Somewhere overhead, a mortar screamed and exploded, flinging shards of stone and earth. A young man beside him, a boy really, grabbed at Peter's uniform, his face pleading for help. Peter pressed a shaking hand to the boy's wound, though he knew it was already too late. His ears rang with the fury of cannon fire.

And just as quickly as it had appeared, the vision receded. The office returned.

Peter stood with eyes locked on the heavy book lying on the floor. He swallowed hard, chest rising and falling. With an unsteady hand, he reached into his coat pocket and retrieved a small silver pill container. Clicking the lid open, he shook two white pills into his palm, and tossed them into his mouth, swallowing dry.

Observing this, Hobbs leaned toward a delivery boy and whispered, "Morphine pills. He was never the same after he came back."

"Came back from where?" the boy asked.

"From hell," Hobbs replied.

Taking a deep breath, Peter gathered himself and walked away, as the bustle of activity returned in the main office.

That evening, the firm of Cratchit and Sons was transformed for the business Christmas party. Desks were pushed aside to make room for a dance floor. The sounds of a violin, accordion, and mandolin mingled joyfully throughout the room. Boughs of holly and sprigs of ivy adorned the walls and door frames, while strings of paper garlands looped from beam to beam. A few candles, placed safely in sconces, lent a warm flicker to the festivities. Laughter and spirited conversation bounced from wall to wall. Punch and mulled wine flowed freely, while a small feast (which included one cooked cod) was laid out on two desks shoved together.

Cratchit, a napkin stuffed into his collar, stood beside the refreshments, indulging in his third pastry of the evening, each one chased with a glass of spiked punch. He was in particularly high spirits when Mary approached and wished him a Merry Christmas.

"Can I get you some tea, Mr. Cratchit?" she asked gently, her eyes flicking to the nearly empty glass in his hand.

"Thank you, but I'm quite content with the punch," he replied, refilling his glass. "By the by—have you seen my laudanum? I must have misplaced it."

Mary smiled and withdrew from her handbag the small blue bottle she had filled with water. "I picked up a new one for you this morning."

He accepted it as if greeting an old friend. "What would I do without you, Mary?"

"You'd live," she replied. "Just not nearly as well."

She pulled the napkin out of his collar and wiped a smudge of raspberry jam from his chin. "Is Tim not yet back from his trip?" she asked, looking over the crowd of merrymakers.

Before Cratchit could respond, a familiar voice rang out from across the room, "Why, there's the old codger now!"

Tim Cratchit entered with the exuberance of a young man whose easy, radiant smile seemed untouched by sorrow. There was no trace of the sickly child he had once been—the frail boy who, for the first decade of his life, had teetered on the edge of the grave. Now twenty-one, he moved with the effortless grace of one wholly confident in the welcome of the world. On either arm clung a young lady—Frieda and Lucy by name—both arrayed more for admiration than modesty, and perfectly pleased to share his favor.

"Tim!" Cratchit beamed, embracing him warmly. "How was Ireland?"

"Quite memorable," Tim replied. "Our clients took me hunting for wild boar."

Frieda leaned in, curious. "And did any of you shoot a boar?"

"Ah, well that depends," Tim said, smiling broadly. "Father, would you consider Mr. Briarwood a bore?"

Cratchit chuckled. "I've been known to doze off in many a conversation with him, yes."

"In that case," Tim replied, "Mr. Flynn did indeed bag a bore that day. A bore's bottom, to be precise. Filled it full of buckshot."

"You mean Mr. Flynn shot his partner in the—" Cratchit patted both his hands against his rear.

"Cheeks? Buttocks? Fanny? Yes!" Tim confirmed as the group around them erupted in laughter. He reached into his satchel, and pulled out a stack of loose papers, handing them to his father. "The signed documents. And hello, what have we here?"

Tim reached back into his satchel, withdrawing a bottle with theatrical flair. "A bottle of the finest whiskey in all Ireland," he declared, offering it to Cratchit. "Merry Christmas, Father."

Cratchit took the bottle with both hands, visibly touched. He pulled his son into another embrace.

Steps away, Peter stood beside his pregnant wife, who rested her hand on the swell of her belly. His smile was forced as he observed his father and Tim together—how easily everything seemed to come for his younger brother!

Cratchit turned his attention to Tim's companions. "And did you bring these two lovely ladies back with you as well?"

"Actually," Tim said with a grin, "I met them on the train."

"In the sleeping carriage," Frieda added.

"Although there wasn't much *sleeping* at night, now was there?" Lucy chimed in, earning some appropriate oohs from those around them.

"I hope you don't mind that I invited them to the party," Tim said to his father.

"Mind?" Cratchit replied, taking the ladies' hands in his. "Why, I'm delighted they're here!"

On the second-floor gallery above the private offices, Belinda stood staring out one of the large picture windows, silhouetted against the silver light of winter moonrise. She wore a soft blue silk gown with fitted sleeves of fine netting, gathered at the wrists with ribbon. Her locks of golden hair had been left down for the occasion, cascading over her shoulders in soft waves.

She heard footsteps on the stairs behind her. The sharp strike of leather soles on wood gave way to the hush of carpet. The steps drew closer, and a man quietly appeared beside her. Neither looked at the other; their eyes remained fixed on the starry London sky.

"A full moon tonight," said Randall, Cratchit's clerk.

"It's beautiful," she replied.

They stood in silence for a moment before he continued, "Romeo swore by the moon his eternal love to Juliet."

His fingers brushed hers, then gently took her hand. She did not pull away.

"Yes," she countered, "but Juliet insisted he use something more consistent than the ever waxing and waning moon to swear by."

Randall grinned and turned to her, leaning in close to her ear.

"It did not end well for them, you know," he whispered.

Belinda finally turned to look at him, a wry smile on her face. "Yet people are still talking about their undying love to this day, aren't they?"

Without pretense or hesitation, Belinda kissed him. Not a stolen kiss, nor a dramatic one, but the quiet, familiar kind exchanged only between those well acquainted with one another's hearts.

Belinda and Randall had met precisely one year ago, on this very spot. In that time, their relationship had blossomed: without secrecy, without scandal, and with her family's gentle blessing.

Randall was the son of a rising Bengali merchant and an Englishwoman. They had met in London during the businessman's dealings abroad. His father loved her—just not enough to renounce the expectations of caste and kin. A marriage had already been arranged for him in Calcutta, and to that duty he returned.

His mother, Elizabeth Yates, lacked wealth, but God had graced her with wisdom and wit. She had raised Randall alone in quiet dignity, aided by little more than a stipend from his father, who visited when commerce brought him to England.

Randall had never set foot in India, nor sought to learn the language. Though affable and educated, he found many doors in London quietly closed. He was not quite English, not quite Indian. That made no difference to Peter Cratchit, who hired him without hesitation. A month later, at the firm's Christmas gathering, Randall met the woman he now held tightly in his arms.

"Happy anniversary, darling," he said, breaking their embrace.

Belinda smiled and asked, "What do you think brought us together, Randall—fate or chance?" (She had a peculiar habit of testing his devotion in the most innocent of ways).

"The Fates never leave love to chance," he said.

She nodded approvingly. "William Shakespeare?"

"No," he replied. "Randall Yates."

Belinda raised her brows, impressed, and took his arm. They began walking slowly toward the stairway.

"Have you responded to your father's letter?" she asked.

Just days ago, a troubling letter had arrived from Calcutta. Randall's father had arranged a marriage for him, one meant to restore the honor his son's birth had tarnished. In return, he would be named heir and placed in charge of the family firm's London division. Like his father before him, Randall was being asked to choose between duty and desire.

"Yes," he responded, "I told my father that I'd be *delighted* to marry a woman I've never met and would be on the next train to India."

Belinda burst into laughter and had to cover her mouth. "I do hope that I shall be invited to the wedding!"

Randall feigned surprise. "Did I not mention that he would like *you* to be the maid of honor?"

She laughed again, uninhibited, as though something tightly wound within her had been granted a moment's reprieve. As they stopped at the top of the stairway, Randall's voice took on a more serious tone. "And how are things with *your* father? Better?"

"Wonderful!" she lied. "We had a most pleasant talk at breakfast this morning."

"Splendid," Randall said, though his tone carried a note of doubt. He hesitated before asking, "And—your arms?"

The light in her eyes dimmed, but only for a moment. The mandolin player announced the first dance of the evening and Belinda's face quickly brightened. She grabbed Randall's arm and they began walking down the stairs as the musicians struck up a new tune.

"I don't mean to cut our conversation short," she said, searching the room, "but Father promised me the first dance—"

Her words caught in her throat—for there, waltzing with one of Tim's companions, was her father. Her smile faded, and she gripped Randall's arm a little tighter. A hush settled over her, and tears welled in her eyes.

On the main floor, Mary smoothed the front of her dress with a measured hand before walking over to Tim. Upon seeing her approach, he smiled broadly. "Mary!"

"Merry Christmas, Tim," she said, and with sudden boldness, leaned forward and kissed him on the cheek. Tim blinked, startled. Mary quickly pointed upward. "Mistletoe," she explained, laughing.

Tim looked up to see the fresh sprig of mistletoe, then back at Mary with a quizzical expression. "I'm not familiar with that tradition."

Mary stopped laughing abruptly. "You—Oh—I hope I didn't—What I mean is—" she stammered, flustered. Not able to contain himself, Tim burst into raucous laughter. Realizing he'd played a fine trick on her, Mary gave him a not-so-gentle shove.

"Shame on you, Tim Cratchit! That was not amusing in the least!"

She turned her back on him, not out of annoyance, but to hide the smile she couldn't quite suppress. She delighted in their teasing remarks and conversations that danced just on the edge of flirtation. With Tim, nothing was ever fully spoken, which both excited and unnerved her. She knew his type: charming, elusive, far too handsome for his own good. But Mary had made up her mind. One day, Tim Cratchit would be hers—not through chance or wishful thinking, but by the quiet force of her resolve.

"Don't sulk, Mary," Tim said, retrieving a small white box from his coat. "I have something for you." Mary turned her head, her curiosity piqued. Tim opened the box and withdrew a tiny clover, holding it up for Mary to see.

"Nu, nu! A four-leaf clover!" she said, delighted.

"From Ireland," Tim confirmed, "just as you asked."

"However did you find one?"

"One?" Tim said. "Why Mary, while traveling to Galway, I fell upon a glen that was covered with them! Someday I'll take you to the very spot."

From across the room, Lucy, one of Tim's train companions, watched their interaction with jealous eyes. She sauntered across the floor and snatched Tim's arm. "How about a dance, luv?" she purred, then leaned over to Mary and whispered in her ear, "Little wonder why they stopped calling him *Tiny* Tim."

As Lucy led Tim away, Mary opened an oval locket on the gold chain around her neck, carefully put the clover inside, closed it, and pressed it to her chest.

On the wooden floor, Tim and Lucy spun with infectious energy, swept along by the spirited strains of a popular English folk song. The air rang with the stamping of boots and the clapping of hands in time with the music.

Lucy moved with grace and flair, the hem of her skirt catching the air, each step a flourish learned from years on music hall stages. Tim matched her enthusiasm, his movements bold yet unrefined. The crowd formed a circle around the two dancers, who grinned like schoolchildren, reveling in the attention.

Midway through the tune, Tim stopped just long enough to ask the violinist for his instrument. Chuckling, the musician handed it over.

Tim tucked the violin beneath his chin, and without missing a beat, joined in the band's song, "The Keel Row." The tune rang out with sprightly charm, and Frieda, seizing the moment, joined the two of them dancing.

As Lucy and Frieda twirled, Tim played beside them, his bow darting across the strings skillfully. He motioned to the crowd, urging them to join in singing.

Gradually, voices filled the room. First a few, then many, until all the guests were singing the jaunty refrain of "The

Keel Row." Tim conducted the partygoers, flourishing his violin bow like a baton.

The song ended in a jubilant crescendo, and the crowd erupted in cheers. Breathless but exhilarated, the three performers took a well-deserved bow. And for that fleeting moment, on that Christmas Eve night, all seemed right with the world.

Cratchit searched the room for Belinda, stopping Randall to inquire after her.

"She left a short while ago," Randall replied, offering the gentlest excuse he could muster. "She said she was exhausted."

Cratchit gave a dry chuckle. "Worn out, is she? From tidying up the house? Try running a business, *that's* exhaustion. Signing papers, keeping workers happy, rising at the ungodly hour of seven."

"Your daughter is up by five," his clerk interjected. But before Randall could press his point, Cratchit had stepped unsteadily onto a crate.

"Attention! Attention, everyone!" he said, raising his voice above the noise. The crowd quickly stilled. "I will be brief," said Cratchit. "If there's one thing I believe it's this: Life's too short for long speeches."

"Nonsense, Father," Tim said. "As president of this firm, it is your *right* to spoil our fun!"

The partygoers erupted in laughter. Like a fire brigade line passing buckets of water to a blaze, a cup of punch made its way from hand to hand, each man and woman taking care not to spill a drop. As the last man on the line, Tim handed the fresh glass of punch to his father, who accepted it with a wink.

"I want to thank every one of you for all that you do," Cratchit said, his tone shifting to one of genuine gratitude. "Truly. It's been another prosperous year for Cratchit and Sons. Wouldn't you agree, Peter?"

"The figures speak for themselves," Peter responded from the back of the room.

"You didn't answer my question," Cratchit said.

"I'm well aware of that!"

The laughter came louder, more robust.

"Are you saying we can't afford this Christmas party? Perhaps we should pass around a hat for donations." Cratchit leaned toward the crowd confidentially, lowering his voice. "That's why I always wear a rather large hat."

His remark elicited yet another round of appreciative laughter from the room. Cratchit lifted his glass and raised his voice for all to hear. "I invite you to eat heartily and drink freely," he said. "A very merry Christmas to us all! God bless us!"

"God bless us, every one," Tim echoed, lifting his glass as well.

All around the room, glasses clinked, and voices repeated the toast. The celebration soared. But gradually, a hush settled over the revelers, as though a sudden draft had entered the room. One by one, heads turned to observe the stranger who stood in the doorway.

It was the soldier.

Silent and uncertain, he had attempted to make himself presentable: combed hair, face scrubbed clean—though unshaven, his uniform still tattered but washed. He surveyed the crowd awkwardly, head lowered, aware that all eyes were on him.

Cratchit, still atop his crate, stepped down and started toward the soldier, but a hand caught his arm.

"It's all right, Father," Peter said gently. Peter passed through the parting crowd with quiet authority. He came to the stranger and offered his hand. "You are most welcome here, friend."

The soldier regarded him for a moment, then reached out slowly and clasped his hand in a firm shake. The musicians resumed their playing, and the conversation returned like the tide.

"Outside, you asked my regiment," the soldier said to Peter. "It was Highland. The 93rd."

Peter's brow lifted, his expression one of recognition and respect. "Ah, The Thin Red Line." He paused before adding, "I was Household Division. Coldstream Guards."

The soldier's face showed awareness and appreciation.

"Well, then," he said, straightening his body and raising his hand in salute.

Peter pulled his shoulders back and returned the soldier's salute. They lowered their arms together slowly in unison.

"Thankfully, the war is over." Peter said, handing the soldier a glass of punch.

"For most," the soldier replied. "Not for all of us."

Peter nodded solemnly in response. They raised their glasses, not in celebration, but in remembrance—to England unbroken, and to their absent brothers in arms whose boots would never touch her soil again.

As the musicians played and the dancers reclaimed the floor, Cratchit slipped quietly out a rear door, unnoticed by all, a shadow receding from the light.

Late that evening, Cratchit, Hawkins, Quill, and Ramsey staggered along the cobblestones—laughing, singing, their breath rising like steam from overworked horses. Only Thatch remained silent, his eyes sharp. As they passed a bank building, his gaze fell on a homeless man lying in the entryway alcove, wrapped in a blanket of damp newspaper.

In that instant, an image seized him: Thatch saw himself as a younger man, curled in a fetal position on the freezing, filthy tile floor of a barred cell. He was barefoot, head shaven, limbs trembling inside a threadbare smock. The cold gnawed at his bones. Hunger scraped from within.

Blinking away the memory, Thatch glanced down at his pocket watch and turned to his companions.

"The hour is late, gentlemen," he said, voice sharp and deliberate. "So, I bid you all a pleasant good night. Tomorrow, we make merry again."

The others raised slurred farewells and retreated into the night. Cratchit lingered, withdrawing the silver flask Belinda had filled for him from his coat pocket. He looked back to see Thatch shrug off his black frock coat and drape it gently over the sleeping man.

It was a small act, done with no audience, no expectation. It stirred something deep in Cratchit: a quiet affirmation that he had placed his trust in the right men.

Reflecting on the moment, Cratchit lifted the flask to his lips and drank. The burn of the liquor was swift and warm. He wiped his mouth with the back of his glove and exhaled.

He walked for many blocks, the fog thickening until the gas lamps became little more than smudges of gold in the gloom. At last, he found himself in the heart of Seven Dials, where seven narrow lanes spilled into a grimy wedge of gin shops, lodging houses, and secondhand stalls. He turned slowly in a circle, peering down each crooked passage.

Then, without hesitation, he chose the darkest road.

With each step, the scent of lavender oil and jasmine grew stronger. His eyes darted furtively from side to side as he heard whispers floating from the shadows: soft, seductive, coaxing. Female voices promising pleasure, like the sirens who lured Odysseus to ruin.

Of the ladies themselves, he caught only fleeting glimpses. An ankle arched above a laced boot, its scarlet stocking rolled just high enough to scandalize. The exaggerated curve of a corset straining against its laces. A pale, bare shoulder exposed beneath a silk mantilla. A garter, rose-pink against white petticoats, glimpsed for the barest moment.

This was not a part of London where respectable gentlemen ventured. It was a warren of shuttered windows, crooked eaves, and doors that rarely opened to the daylight. A quarter where inhibitions vanished, and reputations were lost.

At last, he reached the door, pitch black and narrow, recessed into the wall. Nailed just above it, half-hidden beneath the lintel, hung a single sprig of dried heather, purple and withered. A charm, perhaps, or a ward meant to turn weak-willed men away.

Cratchit looked down at the scarf he was wearing, the one that his wife had made him, and took it off, jamming it into his coat pocket. He raised his hand and knocked on the door three times, slow and deliberate. A pause. Then, the sound of footsteps within.

The door creaked open, releasing a sliver of light. From behind the door came a woman's voice, quiet and blunt.

"It's late."

Without speaking, Cratchit reached into his coat and withdrew a small leather pouch. He shook it once. The coins within gave a soft clink. The door opened wider, and Cratchit entered.

The air hung heavy inside the flat with the earthy scents of sandalwood and frankincense. Feathers, bones, and talismans swayed gently from the ceiling beams. Dozens of amber glass jars with exotic herbs lined the shelves. Candles dripping with wax stood sentry throughout the cluttered room, illuminating ancient books and walls draped in indigo cloth.

Cratchit sat hunched at a table before a fire that popped and spat in the hearth. Opposite him was Katura, a spiritualist from Trinidad by way of a dozen ports. Her skin was the color of aged mahogany; her fingers, ringed in silver, moved with a dancer's grace. Auburn curls, swept back from her face, shimmered in the lamplight. A deep crimson gown, high-collared and finely tailored, lent her an air of quiet authority.

She dressed the part of a lady—not to deceive, but to disarm. In a world ruled by appearances and prejudice, trust came more easily when wrapped in elegance. So she wore it like armor.

Some called her a charlatan. Others, a seer. She let them wonder. The truth, like the dead, revealed itself only to those who listened.

With a skilled hand, she lifted the top tarot card from her worn deck and laid it beside the other cards already arranged before them.

"It's Christmas Eve, Robert," she said, her voice deep, orphic, and laced with Caribbean Creole. "Why aren't you home with your family?"

Cratchit finished taking a drink from his flask and set it on the table. "You claim to be a mystic. Why ask questions when you already know the answers?"

She smiled, then threw her head back in a throaty, unrestrained laugh that filled the room.

"Touché," she replied with a grin. "Isn't that what the French say?"

"I wouldn't know," Cratchit mumbled. "I only know they make horrible porridge."

Katura drew another card, her copper bangles softly jangling as they slid down her arm. She studied Cratchit's face as if it, too, were a card to be read.

"I think you come here not to discern the future, but to escape the present," she said. He remained silent, eyeing his flask and wondering whether it was time for another taste.

"Your wife left you," she recalled. His jaw twitched upon hearing the words. "Do you wish to lose your daughter as well?"

"My wife will beg me to take her back," he declared. "Mark my words."

Katura placed another card on the table. "My husband was a stubborn man like you."

"You left him?" Cratchit asked.

"I poisoned him," she replied. "But that's a story for another time."

She drew the final card, and placed it down with unusual slowness, staring at it coldly. Cratchit leaned forward, impatient for her to speak. "What is it?"

The Death Card stared back at them in silence.

From the darkened corners of the room, a withered hand emerged, its skin shriveled, fingers blackened and curling. Just as its decrepit fingers opened wide to clutch Katura's shoulder, it vanished, so that when she turned her head, there was nothing there.

Then came the whispers.

Soft at first, like the rustle of dry leaves in a graveyard, they coiled through the room. Curling around the ceiling beams, slithering under doorways. Barely audible words, then clearer—insistent. Names. Accusations. Pleas. Laughter. Cries.

Chains began to rattle. A single clink, then a rising clamor of dragging metal, as though great iron links were being pulled across the floor.

The shadows were no longer confined to the walls. They slithered across the floor and rose, stretching into twisted, skeletal forms. Figures with hollow eyes and gaping mouths. They danced without music, their limbs jerking and bending at impossible angles, gliding through the room in a macabre ballet.

Katura stared in amazement. Cratchit followed her gaze, but saw only the vapor of his own breath, as the temperature in the room had plummeted. The fire in the hearth still burned, though it produced no heat.

Faces began to appear—there and gone in an instant. Gaunt. Weeping. Writhing. The air was filled with a loud, keening wail that came from no human throat, but from the dissonant chorus of the dead.

And then, as if the room itself exhaled a final, shuddering breath, all the flames in the room—the hearth, the candles, the lamps—were extinguished all at once, leaving only wisps of smoke and the smell of brimstone. The only illumination that remained was the moonlight slicing through the windows. And silence fell, sudden and crushing.

Katura spied Cratchit's flask, grabbed it, and took a long pull. Deep in thought, she wiped her lips and set it back on the table without looking at him.

"Well?" he demanded, his voice cracking.

"Robert," she said, "Who is Benjamin?"

Cratchit blinked. "Benjamin? I don't know a Benjamin."

"You will," she insisted. "This man—will change your destiny."

She looked down again at the Death Card, her brow furrowing. "Did you hear the chains?" she asked.

"I heard nothing," Cratchit replied.

She drew her shawl tight across her shoulders. "The spirits—they were here for *you*, Robert."

A chill rippled down Cratchit's spine. "To harm me?" he asked.

Katura shook her head. "To *warn* you. They kept whispering 'The secret lies in the ledgers.'"

Cratchit stiffened.

"The secret lies in the ledgers," she repeated.

Surging to his feet, Cratchit knocked the table over, sending tarot cards flying. "Stop saying that!" he shouted at Katura. "You speak nonsense!"

Flushed with drink and shaking with fear, he felt himself coming undone—watched, judged, betrayed by forces he couldn't comprehend. He grabbed an iron poker from the hearth and pointed it at her, as if challenging her to a duel. She met his anger with perfect stillness.

"This is trickery!" he yelled. "A parlor game. A carnival ruse. There are no supernatural forces at work here!"

Suddenly, the poker tore from his hand, flew across the room, and embedded itself in the plaster wall by the hearth.

"Someone begs to differ with you," she said. She rose and quietly set the overturned table back on its legs.

"How—how did you do that?" he stammered, pointing at the poker buried in plaster.

"You must leave now," she insisted.

"What else did you hear?" he asked. She didn't answer. As she turned away, he grabbed her arm. *"What else did they say?"* he demanded.

In the blink of an eye, she twisted Cratchit's wrist downward and slammed his palm against the table. He saw the flash of a stiletto knife before she buried it in the wood between his fingers. He looked down. A single drop of blood trickled from his knuckle to the table.

"Next time you touch me," she warned, "you lose a finger. If you're lucky, I'll let you choose which one."

Cratchit withdrew his hand, rubbing it protectively as he dropped into the chair again. Katura retrieved her knife from the table, folded the blade, and slid it back into the sash at her waist. Cratchit looked up at her, as if waking from a fever dream, his senses dulled, his mind racing.

"They spoke of three spirits," she said, crossing to the hearth. "Heed the first two, and fear the third." Her hand closed tightly around the embedded poker. "They said the first of the three spirits would come to you—*tonight.*"

She pulled the poker from the wall and began prodding the logs.

"I don't believe in ghosts," Cratchit said.

Katura turned her head slowly to look back at him. "You will."

She drove the poker into the logs one final time, and the fire roared back to life.

STAVE TWO

Shadows of the Past

The offices of Cratchit and Sons lay cloaked in a heavy stillness, broken only by the steady tick of a tall grandfather clock positioned along the far wall, its glass face gleaming dimly in the moonlight. The room was still scattered with remnants of the Christmas party: ribbons, empty glasses, a forgotten string of bells. The heavy door had been bolted shut, a wooden chair wedged beneath the handle. It was a crude barrier, but it offered a fragile sense of security.

Cratchit kept vigil, watching the door from a leather chair in front of the fireplace. A tumbler of bourbon rested in his hand. In the other, gripped with white-knuckled resolve, he held an old flintlock pistol—an heirloom he'd never fired.

His cane leaned against the marble hearth within easy reach. He had begun carrying one years ago as a mark of stature and success—the proper accoutrement of a fine gentleman. Lately, its polished silver handle had offered another service, lending strength to legs not so spry as they once were. And now, he reasoned, it might serve as a weapon should the pistol fail him.

As the clock's minute hand reached the apex of its slow march, a sharp *clang* broke the silence. One o'clock. Cratchit looked up at the clock, nerves taut. From beneath the door, a light appeared—soft at first, then intensifying until it bled across the floor in an unearthly glow. The string of bells stirred and chimed softly, as if announcing an arrival.

Suddenly, with a loud *snap*, the bolts on the door sprang open of their own accord. The wooden chair clattered backward. The door creaked open, slowly and deliberately, revealing a blinding white radiance that poured into the room, casting harsh shadows.

Shielding his eyes with one trembling hand, Cratchit raised the pistol with the other. "Who's there?" he demanded, his voice cracking. "What do you want?"

The light began to dim, not extinguishing but refining itself—drawing inward until it revealed a figure standing quietly at its heart. The visitor was ethereal in form, neither man nor woman, clothed in a plain white tunic that fell in folds like moonlight over still water. A shimmering belt encircled its waist. Sandaled feet, clean and bare, hovered an inch above the ground.

But it was the light that truly defined it.

The aura around it was alive—breathing, blooming, glowing. A corona of color that flickered and danced. An ever-shifting tapestry of hue and mood that morphed at will: now pale gold, now deep violet, now forest green.

"I am the Ghost of Christmas Past," said the Spirit, stepping forward with a voice both youthful and ancient.

"Why are you here?" asked Cratchit meekly.

The Ghost began, "I am here to show you—"

Crack! The pistol went off. The stray bullet passed through the Ghost and struck the grandfather clock, shattering its faceplate. Glass, gears, and springs burst outward, and its pendulum dropped with a heavy thud.

Cratchit blinked, looking down at the smoking pistol in his hand, dumbfounded.

"Are you trying to get rid of me?" asked the Spirit, unfazed. "Or are you just—

It looked over at the shattered clock.

"—killing time?"

Cratchit stammered a weak apology: "I—It—I didn't mean to—"

The Ghost extended its arm, and the pistol instantly leapt from Cratchit's grip into the Spirit's hand. With unsettling calm, the Ghost turned the weapon on Cratchit.

"They say your life flashes before your eyes just before you die," it mused. "Let's see if they're right."

"Spirit! What are you—"

Crack! The pistol fired once more with a deafening blast. But this time, halfway to its destination, the bullet slowed dramatically. Frozen in place, Cratchit focused on the bullet moving ever so slowly, but ever so inexorably toward him.

The Ghost's aura changed to a celestial blue. "What do you see, Bob Cratchit?"

As Cratchit stared, transfixed, at the bullet, all else in the room faded: sight, sound, and sensation. "I see—I see my family!" he said in astonishment. "In our old house!"

Cratchit stood on a snow-covered cobblestone street, gazing through the window of his former home in Camden Town. Through the frosted pane, a familiar scene unfolded, warm and bright against the bitter cold outside. It was

Christmas Eve thirteen years ago, and the Cratchit home bustled with laughter and light. There was his younger self, not yet forty, seated at the head of the table, animated and glowing with youthful cheer. His wife Abigail stirred a pot near the hearth. Martha and Belinda, still young slips of girls, flitted from one task to another, tying ribbons, setting plates. Peter, fourteen and full of pride, wore his father's oversized shirt collar. The youngest children dashed between chairs in gleeful pursuit, while Tiny Tim—feeble but grinning—sat near the fire, his delicate form leaning on his little crutch.

As the Ghost and Cratchit passed unseen into the room, Cratchit instinctively fell to one knee and opened his arms wide.

"Abigail! Peter! Belinda!" he cried, his voice breaking with joy. He was puzzled when no one seemed to hear him. "Martha! James! Jenny!" But there was still no response from his family.

His eyes fell on his youngest son, who stared intently at the fire in the hearth. "Tim?" Cratchit whispered, his heart breaking. "Why don't you answer?"

The Spirit turned to him gently. "They can't see or hear you. They are but shadows of things past."

Cratchit's arms fell slowly to his sides—empty. He and the Ghost watched as his former self pulled over a chair for Tiny Tim and guided the boy into it with tender care. Then, taking his own seat next to Tim at the table, he bowed his head.

"Father," Bob prayed, his voice solemn, "thank you for the bountiful feast you set before us. May it nourish our bodies, bringing health and healing."

He reached for Tim's frail hand, clasping it gently in his own. "Bless this family, and may the love we share today grow stronger with every day that passes. Amen."

"Amen," came the chorus from the others, while Cratchit, standing in the corner of the room, echoed the word with reverence.

The Spirit regarded him. "Is something wrong?"

Cratchit shook his head faintly. "No. Nothing. Only—it would have been pleasant for all of us to be together *this* Christmas."

At the table, the younger Bob raised his glass. "To Mr. Scrooge, the Founder of this Feast!"

Mrs. Cratchit snorted. "Mr. Scrooge?! I'll not drink to the health of such a stingy, hard-hearted man, Robert."

"Abigail—the children. Christmas Day," Bob said gently, a quiet reprimand.

"You know he is," she insisted. "Nobody knows it better than you do."

Cratchit nodded. "She's quite right. That man was as cold as flint. But then, the strangest thing happened. He changed—overnight! On that Christmas Day, he was—"

"—filled with the Christmas spirit?" the Ghost said, finishing his thought.

Cratchit turned in surprise. "Yes! How did you—?"

A sudden stillness settled over him. His brow furrowed, and he took a step back, blinking at the Spirit as if seeing things clearly for the first time.

"*You* appeared to Ebenezer that Christmas, didn't you?"

The Spirit only smiled.

"Are you trying to change *me* as well?" Cratchit demanded. "But why, Spirit? I am no slave to money!"

"There are temptations other than money," the Ghost replied, "that destroy a man's character—and enslave a man's soul."

Cratchit squared his shoulders with heated pride. "I'm quite content with who I am and the way I am! I am no skinflint. No miser. No misanthrope. I am no *Scrooge*!"

"Bob!"

The voice came from behind him. Cratchit turned, and his heart skipped a beat.

"Ebenezer!" he whispered.

The setting had changed again. In the familiar counting house of Scrooge and Marley stood Ebenezer Scrooge. His waistcoat was dark maroon twill, his silver hair neatly combed, and his expression aglow with the kindness and clarity of a soul redeemed.

After Scrooge's transformation, the office had undergone a renewal of its own. Ebenezer had insisted upon it! Though still modest in its furnishings, it was a far cry from the place of bitter cold and greyness it had once been. Where once drafts and darkness clung to the corners, now there was firelight and warmth. A freshly laid rug muffled the creak of the boards. Polished brass inkwells gleamed on orderly desks. The windows, scrubbed clean, drank in the morning sun.

"How are you this morning, Bob?" he called out cheerily. "Well, I hope?"

For a fleeting moment, Cratchit thought the greeting was meant for him. But as Scrooge walked toward him, he passed clean through as if he were mist. Cratchit turned and once again saw himself, a few years older than before, seated at the clerk's desk—a brightness in his eyes, a looseness in his shoulders, a smile that broke freely across his face.

"Quite well, Mr. Scrooge!" Bob replied, rising from his chair, scarcely able to contain himself. He was so anxious to tell Ebenezer the glorious news that he had hardly slept.

"Last night," he said, breath quickening, "we received the most wonderful surprise. Tiny Tim—he *walked* into the room. Without his crutch!" Bob's voice cracked, and tears gathered at the corners of his eyes. "He walked on his *own two legs*!"

Scrooge was struck silent. "A miracle," he murmured at last. "But—I knew he would."

"The doctors say he's growing stronger every day," Bob continued.

"Excellent, Bob. Excellent," said Scrooge, eyes glistening as he put a reassuring hand on his clerk's shoulder. He walked past Bob to look out the window, overcome with emotion.

"And it's all thanks to your generosity, Mr. Scrooge," Bob said, grateful beyond measure. "It never would have happened without you."

As Cratchit watched, the full weight of his former self's words settled over him. He now regretted shouting at the Spirit just moments ago. Had the Ghosts not come that night, Scrooge would never have changed. And Tim would never have walked—indeed, might not have lived another year. The fruits of that divine intervention were undeniable: a son saved, a family spared, a future rewritten.

Scrooge turned from the window, taking a long breath. "Bob, I've been thinking about expanding the business."

"Expanding, sir?" Bob repeated, puzzled.

“Yes,” said Scrooge, stepping closer. “We’ve outgrown this place. And you've outgrown your position.” Bob blinked, not yet grasping the full meaning.

Scrooge continued: “What I’m trying to say is—I want *you* to be my new partner, Bob Cratchit.”

Bob stood motionless, eyes wide. “I—I don’t know what to say,” he stammered.

“Just say you’ll do it,” Scrooge said, his eyes twinkling, “and I’ll have the signs changed tomorrow to read ‘Scrooge and Cratchit.’”

“Mr. Scrooge—” Bob began, crossing to him.

“Ebenezer,” the older man corrected gently, offering his hand.

Bob looked at Scrooge’s outstretched hand, grasped it with both hands and shook it vigorously.

“Thank you, sir,” Bob said, barely able to contain his emotions. “I’ll never forget this. I’ll always be in your debt.”

“And how did you repay that debt?” asked the Ghost.

Cratchit bowed his head, his expression collapsing into regret. “Take me home, Spirit,” he said hoarsely. “I’ve seen enough.”

The Ghost made no reply, but silently raised its arm. They were instantly back at Cratchit’s place of business. The bullet was now closer to Cratchit, who stood immobile, his fear mounting.

“Spirit—why can I not move?” he asked with growing alarm.

“Because I’ve slowed time,” explained the Ghost patiently. “You and the bullet now exist within the same suspended moment. One that would otherwise pass in the blink of an eye.”

The Ghost's aura flickered, shifting to a sea-green hue. Light spilled suddenly through the office windows. Cratchit found himself once more in the past, standing beside the Spirit in the offices of Scrooge and Cratchit.

The firm had moved from the old counting-house to a more commodious space. Though not grand, the premises were respectably appointed—fitting for a business whose affairs had begun to outgrow their humble origins. (This, of course, was *before* Bob Cratchit undertook his elaborate renovations.)

"In a few short years," the Ghost said, "Scrooge had built a small business into a thriving enterprise."

"*Scrooge* built?" scoffed Cratchit. "Have you forgotten that I was his partner?"

Cratchit saw his former self again, older now, sitting at the desk in his office, surrounded by the four businessmen.

"Oh, yes. That's true," the Ghost replied, nodding. "You had begun to believe yourself a man of influence."

Thatch leaned forward with a conspiratorial grin. "So, it's agreed then. You'll join us at the club tonight, Mr. Cratchit, and we'll discuss our business over brandy and cigars."

"Brandy and cigars," Quill repeated with delight. "Capital suggestion!"

"Gentlemen," Bob said, "I heartily agree with your proposals for expansion and investment. And your terms for the loan are very generous. But the risk—"

"Ah, but with risk comes rewards," Ramsey interjected, brushing off Bob's concern.

"Yes, but even if I were willing, I'm certain Ebenezer would be against accepting the loan."

Hawkins leaned in. "That's why we came to *you*. We've heard you're the more *discerning* partner in such matters."

"More forward-thinking," added Ramsey.

Thatch smiled. "I've no doubt our friend here shall one day join the Knights Paragon."

Bob raised an eyebrow. "Knights Paragon?"

In answer, the men each raised a hand, one by one, revealing identical gold rings. Wearing the ring was a silent signal that one *belonged*, not by merit, but by invitation.

"Is that not a secret society?" Bob asked.

Thatch gave a quiet chuckle. "Not secret—just exclusive." With deliberate care, he rested a hand on Bob's shoulder, fixing him with eyes sharp as polished steel. "You were meant to ascend, Bob Cratchit. And rise you shall. With our help, you'll be the envy of your friends and enemies alike."

Bob blinked. "I have no enemies."

"None that you know of, perhaps," Thatch said, gazing toward Scrooge's office. "Your partner was one of the most miserly curmudgeons in all of London. They say he changed in a single night. That may be. But he *hasn't* changed with the times. The world moved on—and he did not."

Thatch leaned closer. His tone softened, intimate now. "Your company needs a man of vision. That man is *not* Ebenezer Scrooge."

He bent low, voice barely above a whisper, lips almost brushing Bob's ear.

"That man is *you*, Bob Cratchit."

His words settled into Bob's mind with quiet weight. Thatch caught a flicker of movement at the edge of his vision. He turned and saw Mary through the glass, staring straight at him. She rose from her desk and started toward the open office door. Thatch gave Ramsey a silent nod. Ramsey seized the handle and, just as Mary reached the threshold, closed the door in her face.

"Tonight, then?" Thatch asked, reaching into his waistcoat and withdrawing a calling card for Bob. Embossed in elegant script were simply the words: "The Excelsior."

The Excelsior's sign was a beacon in the gloom, its gilded letters promising both indulgence and discretion. London's most exclusive gentlemen's club was located in the heart of St. James, where handsome carriages arrived with well-heeled businessmen seeking their sanctum of privilege and pleasure.

Beyond its heavy oak doors lay a cathedral of decadence. Cherrywood paneling lined the walls, reflecting the soft flicker of glass chandeliers that dangled overhead like frozen fireworks. Heavy drapes in wine and gold muffled the outside world, and the smell of cigars and old leather hung thick as incense in a chapel.

Cratchit and the Ghost, its strange color-shifting aura pulsing faintly, observed from the periphery. "They brought you into their circle, made you feel important," said the Spirit. "Just years ago a humble clerk—now, consorting with the city's powerful."

The five men reclined in deep armchairs, a cheroot balanced between their fingers and a brandy snifter warming in their palms. Bob laughed with them, nodded when expected, raised his glass in agreement. He looked, to all appearances, the consummate gentleman.

His gaze drifted to his associates' chalice-emblazoned rings. Surreptitiously, he slid the gold foil band from his cigar onto his finger, imagining what it might feel like to be a Knight.

The Knights Paragon were formed over a century ago by businessmen of exceptional character. Men who held themselves to a higher standard. They chose the chalice as their emblem: a symbol of virtue, temperance, and unity. Their charter spoke of fostering integrity in commerce, promoting strong community values, and elevating the moral fiber of those entrusted with influence.

Over time, a struggle emerged amongst the Knights—between those who held fast to the Order's ideals, and opportunists who sought power for personal gain. Stories surfaced of favors exchanged, laws sidestepped, constables paid to look the other way. Accusations whispered but never proven.

Their reputation did not tarnish; their mission remained intact. England continued to regard the Order as a proud remnant of noble aspirations. They were paragons still.

Cratchit had heard the rumors, of course, but dismissed them as hearsay or envy. The bitter grumblings of men denied a ring. Though he knew precious little about his four associates, he felt confident in their character.

They were, after all, Knights.

Bob realized the men's gold rings were symbols of virtue and honor, but also stature and power. Doors opened to those who wore the chalice. They were men of standing who had earned the respect of their peers. Men of consequence who gathered in rooms few were invited to enter.

At that moment, he knew he wanted to be one of them.

Without warning, the club dissolved into smoke. When it cleared, Cratchit found himself beside the Spirit in a gambling house. The Excelsior's stately serenity had vanished; here, the air crackled with risk and intoxication. His former self stood at a crowded table, sleeves rolled up, eyes sharp with excitement. Dice flew from his hand, danced across the felt, and landed in his favor. Cheers erupted. A porter handed him his winnings, which he pocketed, feeling a flush of exhilaration entirely new to him.

"They introduced you to a world you had never known," said the Spirit, "and included you in all their vices."

The room changed again. They were now in a music hall, alive with motion and sound: all brass and bosoms, tambourines and teasing glances. Bob sat in a velvet booth. Women twirled past in perfumed clouds, their petticoats flashing.

One dancer, bold-eyed and ruby-lipped, lowered herself into his lap and bestowed a kiss, which Bob accepted with scant resistance. The businessmen hooted. Thatch swirled his wine, observing in silence.

From across the table, one of the businessmen opened an expensive bottle of champagne, carelessly popping the cork in Bob's direction. The cork blasted forth as if shot from a gun, then slowed to a spectral crawl, transforming into the bullet. The revelers faded into darkness. Cratchit suddenly found himself alone in the velvet booth, seated where his former self had been just moments before. He was rooted to the spot, limbs paralyzed, eyes fixed on the glimmering bullet inching toward his forehead.

“Make it stop, Spirit,” he said, his voice desperate. *“Make it stop!”*

“I’m sorry, Bob, I can’t,” Cratchit heard Scrooge say. The Ghost’s aura had changed color again and so had his surroundings. Cratchit now stood in the offices of Scrooge and Cratchit, watching his former self argue with Scrooge in his office.

“I simply can’t approve of this investment,” Scrooge continued, his voice firm, his pen laid aside.

“Don’t be blind, Ebenezer!” Bob said. “An opportunity like this may never come again. I insist you reconsider!”

With a forceful push, he closed the door behind him. Their voices became the muffled grumblings of men too often at odds.

A gust of wind blew in as the entrance door opened, and Tim Cratchit, who had just turned seventeen, strode in with the zeal of youth. As he rummaged through papers in the satchel slung over his shoulder, he plowed right into Mary Fielding, sending a flurry of loose papers into the air.

“I’m dreadfully sorry,” Tim said, stooping to pick up the papers.

“No, it was my fault,” Mary replied, kneeling beside him with a grace that caught him off guard. He flashed her a boyish grin as she tucked a stray curl behind her ear.

“Are you here to see someone?” she asked.

“Actually, I’ve just taken a position at this firm.”

“How wonderful,” she said. As they hurriedly collected the last of the papers, they reached for the same invoice, bumping foreheads. Surprise gave way to laughter, as they both plopped down on the floor, rubbing their heads.

"I've read," said Tim, "that touching foreheads is a traditional greeting among the Maori in New Zealand."

"I believe I much prefer the traditional greeting among the English in Great Britain," she said, extending her hand. "Mary Fielding."

He took her hand gently. "Tim. Tim Cratchit."

She lifted her eyebrow in mock surprise. "Fancy that, Master Cratchit. You share the same last name as the owner of the company."

"Yes," Tim said, smiling. "What a remarkable coincidence."

"Would you like me to introduce you?" Mary teased, enjoying their playful jousting.

"You're most kind," he said, leaning closer to her, "but I'd much rather continue *our* introductions."

Raised voices echoed through the glass-paneled wall of Scrooge's office, drawing their attention.

"Is this typical?" Tim asked, as they both stood.

"Of late, it is," she replied, buckling Tim's satchel now that his papers were safe inside. "How is Peter? Any news from your brother?"

"Wounded in battle. Again. Nothing serious, or so he claims."

Heavy booms drew their attention back to the office, where they saw Bob pounding the desk. A moment later, the door burst open, and Bob stormed out and entered his own office, slamming the door with such force the glass rattled.

"You began to resent your partner," the Ghost said.

"We didn't always see eye to eye," Cratchit replied diplomatically.

The Spirit's glow flickered. "Ah yes. You were a man of vision. And he—a relic."

"His mind was not as sharp as it once was, poor fellow," Cratchit insisted.

"You pitied him," said the Spirit.

Cratchit considered the Ghost's assessment and nodded. "I did. Yes, I suppose I did."

The Ghost stepped closer. "Is that why you plotted to remove him from the company?"

Cratchit recoiled. "No. No, Spirit!"

The Ghost's aura changed to magenta as everyone in the office slowly vanished and darkness fell. It was the middle of the night. A single candle flickered on Scrooge's desk.

"Late at night," the Ghost murmured, "long after everyone had gone home, you would steal into Scrooge's office."

Cratchit bristled. "Lies!" he shouted.

"You would open the financial records Ebenezer kept."

"I won't watch these lies!" he shouted again, his voice cracking.

"And by the flickering candlelight, you carefully altered the numbers in *his ledger*."

"Stop! Stop, I beg you!" Cratchit's pleas rang out, but the Spirit pressed forward.

"You made it appear as if Ebenezer's mind was failing. That were it not for your keen eye in discovering his errors, the company would have suffered greatly. All saw you as the savior of the firm. And Scrooge—he was discredited. Unfit. Cast aside."

Cratchit's voice faltered, a whisper now. "I—I didn't do it for myself. It was for the firm."

The Spirit gave no quarter. "You forced him out! Is this the way you repay the man who mentored you?"

"I tell you, I didn't do it for me!" Cratchit cried.

The Ghost's glow shifted again. "The man who made you partner?"

Cratchit could barely speak. "I never meant to harm him!"

"The man who saved your son's life?"

Before Cratchit could protest further, he heard Tim's voice.

"Uncle! Uncle Ebenezer!"

Cratchit turned and found himself on the streets of London once again. Tim raised a gloved hand and waved.

"Hallo!" Scrooge responded, stepping out from a bookshop, his scarf flapping in the winter wind. Tim ran toward him, then playfully slid along an icy patch. Scrooge caught him before he could tumble, and the two burst into laughter.

"Have you heard?" Tim said breathlessly. "Martha's getting married!"

Scrooge's eyes lit up. "You don't say! Well, I shall write to your sister this very day and send her my warmest wishes. So, what brings you into town, Master Cratchit?"

"I'm meeting Father," Tim replied. "He's introducing me to some of his business colleagues—Mr. Thatch, Mr. Hawkins, Mr.—"

Scrooge's smile faltered. "Yes, yes, I know them well, I'm sorry to say."

Tim pressed on. "Father wants me to spend more time getting to know the business. But it's so deadly dull. And I have other interests."

"Then you should pursue them," Scrooge said, thumping Tim's chest gently.

"Father won't allow it," Tim replied, casting his eyes downward. "In years past he used to carry me on his shoulders. Now, I feel like a dog kept on a short lead. What happened to my father, Uncle Ebenezer?"

Scrooge placed a hand on the young man's shoulder. "The *world* happened to him, Tim."

A flower girl no more than eight years of age stepped up to them. Her cheeks were dirty, her hands chapped, and in them she held a single pink carnation.

"Flower, sir?" she asked timidly. "A flower for a halfpenny."

Scrooge looked at her with compassion. Accepting the flower, he reached into his coat and withdrew a coin. "What is your name, child?" he asked gently.

"Alice, sir," she replied. She looked at the coin and shook her head in disappointment. "I'm sorry, sir. I haven't change for a guinea."

Scrooge closed her small fingers around the coin and smiled. "A very Merry Christmas to you, Alice."

The child's eyes lit up. "A whole guinea?! Bless you, sir! Thank you, sir! And a Merry Christmas to you, too, sir!"

She skipped away, elated, as Scrooge laughed in delight. He turned and tucked the flower into Tim's lapel. "Now then," he said, straightening Tim's collar. "For such an important meeting, you want to make a good impression. There!"

Scrooge stepped back to inspect Tim's appearance. His expression shifted, softening with sudden emotion. "Good heavens, Tim," he murmured. "Wasn't it only yesterday that you were Alice's age? When did you become a man?"

Bob peered out from the etched glass window of Fig and Whistle, a polished establishment frequented by businessmen. Upon seeing Tim and Scrooge deep in conversation, he moved swiftly to the door.

"Tim!" Bob called sharply as he emerged into the cold. Tim turned, surprised.

"You're late!" Bob snapped before retreating into the restaurant without so much as a glance at Scrooge.

Scrooge gave Tim a gentle nudge. "Go. We'll talk again soon." Tim nodded and followed his father inside.

"Ebenezer was like a second father to Tim," said the Spirit, its form shimmering faintly in the cold air.

"He loved the old man," Cratchit admitted.

"And you were jealous of that love," the Ghost continued. "You stole your son away from Scrooge at every opportunity."

Tim sat with his father and the businessmen at The Excelsior. He puffed clumsily on a cigar and erupted into a fit of coughing, eliciting hearty laughter from the men.

"I was introducing him to the world of business," Cratchit offered.

The Spirit's voice was reproachful. "A young man had no *business* in the places you took him."

In the velvet-curtained back room of a gambling parlor, Tim rolled dice with the same reckless vigor his father once displayed. Cratchit and the businessmen surrounded him, clapping him on the back, congratulating him on his winning streak.

"There are more deals struck in back rooms than in front offices, I can assure you," said Cratchit.

At a raucous music hall, a dancer teased Tim with silk scarves, then plucked the carnation from his lapel, and tucked it in her hair. Thatch discreetly slipped her a note as she passed by.

Cratchit's voice was resolute. "The world is corrupt. I didn't make it that way. But I've discovered you can't change it. So, if teaching my son to survive is a sin, then curse me for it!"

Suddenly, the music halted. The lights flared. The memory dissolved.

Back in the present, Cratchit and Sons was cloaked in silence. Cratchit still stood frozen, unable to move, the bullet now less than an inch from his forehead.

"Should I lie to my children?" Cratchit sputtered. "Tell them the world is decent and fair, is that what you suggest?"

The Ghost of Christmas Past regarded him coolly. "I suggest you—duck."

Cratchit blinked. "Duck?"

"Now."

The Spirit snapped its fingers as Cratchit hurled himself to the floor. The bullet resumed its natural speed and blasted a splintering hole in the paneling behind him.

"Dodged a bullet that time, eh?" the Spirit quipped, stepping over to Cratchit, who lay shaking on the floor, both arms covering his head. "I'll wager you could use a drink."

When Cratchit lowered his arms, he found himself sitting with the Spirit at the Lion's Head Pub, a tavern frequented by working folk (and by those far too drunk to work). The air reeked of old ale and spilled hopes. It was a place where dreams came to drown.

The barkeep drew beer from a wooden cask and sent a tankard sliding down the bar. Cratchit reached for it—but it passed cleanly through his hand. The tankard continued on, landing neatly in the grip of a serving girl, who vanished into the crowd.

With a wave of its hand, the Spirit summoned a pewter goblet before them.

"*This one* is yours," it said.

Cratchit snatched it eagerly and took a generous gulp—then sputtered, coughing. "Salty," he muttered, eyeing the contents with distaste.

"To remind you of the tears of those you've wronged," said the Ghost.

Cratchit shoved the drink aside just as the tavern door creaked open, letting in a gust of wintry air. Abigail Cratchit stepped inside, bundled tightly in her shawl. Her eyes swept the pub's dim recesses until they found the barkeep polishing a greasy plate with a dirty rag. He saw her and nodded his head to a table in the corner.

A shrill burst of laughter, coarse and high-pitched, echoed from the darkened corner. Her gaze followed the sound until it landed upon Tim and the music hall dancer entangled in a louche embrace. They were kissing, giggling, utterly indifferent to the eyes of the world.

She approached the table stiffly. Tim glanced up, his face flushed with drink and amusement.

"Oh, hello Mother," he said with a lazy smile, as the girl nuzzled his neck. "Mother, I'd like you to meet Fanny."

"Phoebe," the girl corrected, batting her lashes with theatrical innocence.

Tim raised a brow. "Phoebe? Are you quite sure?"

"The hour is late, Tim," Abigail advised her son. "Say good night to your—lady friend."

Tim struggled to stand, bracing himself on the edge of the table. "Ah, but I must walk her home."

Phoebe waved him off. "It's all right, luv. I live upstairs. See you tomorrow, eh?"

She leaned down, kissed his cheek, and rose to go. As she turned, Tim gave her bottom a playful swat. She let out a squeal of delight, wagged a finger at him, and ascended the stairs with exaggerated sway.

Tim slouched back into his seat and bellowed, "Barkeep! Another whiskey!"

"Where have you been all night?" Abigail asked, her voice taut.

"With Father," Tim replied. "And Mr. Thatch—and three other fellows. And Faye."

"Phoebe," she corrected him.

Tim blinked. "Who's Phoebe?" He turned his head and shouted, "Barkeep! Where's my rum?!"

"You've had enough to drink, child," Abigail admonished him.

"I'm not a *child* anymore, Mother!" Tim snapped. "I'm old enough to make remarkably poor decisions on my own."

Though she tried to remain stern, Abigail couldn't help but smile at Tim's humor. "Agreed," she said, easing into the chair beside him. "As long as one of those remarkably poor decisions isn't avoiding your mother."

He nodded. "Agreed."

"Or your father," she added.

Tim hesitated, averting his eyes and looking down at his empty glass.

"Your father would do anything for you," she whispered. "You're his favorite, you know."

"I know," Tim said. "Why does that feel more like a curse than a blessing?" He sighed, struggling to find the words. "The family business means everything to him. It means nothing to me. I hate it."

Abigail showed no hint of judgment, only compassion and concern. "You must tell him how you feel."

"It would kill him," Tim replied.

"It's killing *you*." She put her hand gently on his arm. "Each day I see you slipping further away. You have no idea how much that frightens me." She cupped his chin, coaxing him to meet her eyes. "I nearly lost you once when you were a child. I couldn't bear the thought of losing you again."

Tim looked away. "You'd all be better off without me."

Abigail gasped. "Oh no, no, no, my child, don't say that. Don't say that!" She pulled him close, arms wrapping around him tightly.

He rested his forehead on her shoulder. For a long moment, neither spoke. Her hand came to rest gently at the back of his neck. His shoulders softened, if only slightly, and his eyes closed.

Then, as though hearing his cue to go on stage, he jerked away and rose abruptly. "Ha! But don't worry, Mother!" he said loudly, weaving his way over to the bar. "I'll play the role of the *Good Son*—for the family's sake. *Jovial Tim. Dependable Tim. Good-natured Tim!*" He dropped onto a seat at the bar and slammed his palm on the counter. "Barkeep! Another ale!"

The barkeep glanced over, assessing him with cool disapproval. "You're done," he said.

Tim sat silently, his eyes heavy. "So I am," he agreed, before he tipped forward and passed out, his head thudding onto the bar.

The lights suddenly went out, cloaking the room in darkness.

In the center of the room, a boy of fifteen appeared—transparent, colorless—wearing canvas trousers, a cotton shirt, and a cricket bat slung across one shoulder. His face was alive with laughter, though no sound escaped his lips.

"Seven years ago," said the Ghost, its voice reverent, "your son passed from this world."

Cratchit gazed at the apparition, reliving the memory. "James," he whispered.

"They say he was quite good at cricket."

The boy slowly faded, as a breath caught in Cratchit's throat. "Yes. Yes, he was quite good, indeed."

The room darkened for only a moment before another apparition emerged. This time, a seventeen-year-old girl standing at a fog-shrouded dock, two worn valises in her hands, her raven hair blowing in the salt air.

"Shortly thereafter," said the Ghost, "your youngest daughter ran off to America in secret—with a sailor."

Cratchit's voice cracked. "Jenny."

The girl turned and offered him a bittersweet smile as the vision dissolved. From the Spirit's aura, light bloomed again: long, golden shadows stretching into the dark.

"Losing a child changes a man, does it not?" the Ghost asked gently.

"It does," Cratchit whispered, a tear trailing down his cheek. "It is a wound that never heals."

The Spirit's gaze remained fixed. "James and Jenny were taken from you through no fault of your own. But the fate of your other children—their future—will be yours to answer for."

Cratchit flinched. "But why blame *me*, Spirit?" he asked, his voice fraying. "What family does not suffer the pangs and struggles of life? In *every* man's past there are shadows filled with heartbreak. Why show me *only* the sorrows? What of the celebrations? Why do you keep those from me?"

"Ah, yes. The joyous occasions," said the Ghost. "Observe your daughter's wedding day." The Spirit's aura changed to silver, and with that, the world began to shift again.

The Cratchits' local church swelled up around them. From a perch high in the choir loft, Cratchit and the Spirit looked down upon the sunlit nave. Music soared from the organ, echoing off the stone arches.

In the front pew, Abigail sat closest to the aisle, dabbing at her eyes with a kerchief. Beside her, Peter wore full military dress, his arm in a sling. Then Tim, dashing in formal evening wear. The pews behind them were filled with familiar faces, friends and family alike.

Belinda, glowing with quiet grace, made her way down the aisle as maid of honor. She gave a small, affectionate nod to her family as she passed. Reaching her spot in front, she turned to face the congregation.

Then, at the grand entrance, Martha appeared, looking radiant, her arm looped through her father's. Her wedding gown, fashioned of ivory silk and trimmed with delicate lace, shimmered faintly in the light that streamed through the high stained-glass windows. A row of tiny pearl buttons ran from her neckline to her waist, and a pale satin sash gathered the gown gently at the back. Her veil, edged in fine embroidery, floated behind her. She held a simple bouquet of winter roses and greenery.

"How beautiful she looked!" Cratchit whispered from the loft.

Martha's eyes flicked nervously to her father, who tottered beside her—cheeks flushed, eyes dazed, a lopsided grin across his face.

"And how merry *you* looked," said the Ghost dryly.

Cratchit stiffened. "It was a celebration."

"It was an embarrassment," the Ghost countered.

As they made their way down the aisle, guests turned to watch—and to whisper. A few chuckled; others exchanged pitying glances. The music concluded as they reached the altar, where Martha stopped next to her stoic groom, Thomas Stanhope.

The bespectacled minister opened his well-worn bible, and began the ceremony: "Dearly beloved, we are gathered here—"

A collective gasp rippled through the congregation.

Bob's trousers had slipped to his ankles. He had failed to refasten his braces after visiting the church lavatory—an egregious oversight brought on by too much port at the vicar's table.

"Church feels rather drafty this morning," he whispered to Martha, blissfully unaware that he was standing in only his drawers. Martha closed her eyes and prayed for the floor to swallow her.

From the front row, Abigail urgently tried to get his attention.

He turned his head to look at her, and blinked, oblivious as to why she was whispering his name. She gestured frantically to his legs. Only then did he look down and recognize the problem.

"Well, that's not good," he murmured.

Stooping to retrieve his dignity, he lost his balance and toppled headfirst into a grand floral arrangement. Water splashed. Blooms scattered. A heavy vase shattered against the floor as Bob lay sprawled in the mayhem.

In the choir loft, Cratchit buried his face in his hands.

"You haven't set foot in church since that day," said the Spirit.

"To have everyone glare at me in judgment, whispering behind my back?" Cratchit grumbled. "No thank you."

The Spirit's aura altered to a violet hue, and as it did, the setting became a banqueting hall where the wedding festivities for Martha and Thomas were well underway. Long tables lined the perimeter, draped in fine white linens and set with rented china and polished cutlery. Velvet ribbons and garlands of evergreen had been fastened along the mantel and beams. Candles glowed from every ledge and sill, and the clatter of plates, the occasional burst of laughter, and the scrape of boots on polished floorboards filled the air. A trio of hired musicians—violin, cello, and pianoforte—played elegant waltzes and spirited reels. Guests dined on roast duck and glazed vegetables, and the punch bowl was never left unattended. The room hummed with the warmth of old friends and the joy of new beginnings.

Cratchit and the Ghost surveyed the celebration, and a glow of quiet pride lit Cratchit's face. What matter if the cost of the evening had meant taking on more debt than prudence allowed? Surely a little extravagance could be forgiven in such prosperous times.

Although Bob had spared no effort—or coin—to impress his business associates, they regarded the event with the bored detachment of men accustomed to more opulent affairs.

At a prominent table, Thatch, Hawkins, and Ramsey sat clustered around a half-empty bottle of claret, their spirits flagging as the evening wore on.

"How very fortunate we are," Hawkins said with obvious disdain, "that Mr. Cratchit invited us to the social event of the year."

Ramsey commented that Mr. Quill seemed to be making the best of an insufferable evening, nodding toward the dance floor where Quill, awkward but indefatigable, attempted a spirited waltz with a robust young lady.

"Anywhere there's libations and willing women, our good colleague is right at home," noted Hawkins.

Ramsey grimaced after taking a bite of food. "Did you taste the hors d'oeuvres? The pâté is indigestible, and the petit fours are an affront to the palate—"

"Gentlemen!" Thatch interrupted sharply. "Our host approaches."

Bob, now nearly sober and composed, arrived at their table with a broad smile. Thatch extended his hand.

"Bob! Congratulations, old fellow! It was—an unforgettable wedding."

Ramsey nodded eagerly. "And the food is—perfection! Is it French?"

"Good Lord, I hope not," Bob replied.

Quill stumbled over, clutching his chest in mock distress. "My heart! My heart!"

Bob looked alarmed. "Heavens, man, are you alright?"

Quill collapsed into a chair with a sigh. "I think I'm in *love*."

The group chuckled as Quill's dance partner waved to him coyly from across the room. Quill waved back with a cloth napkin.

Bob's gaze shifted to the sitting room just off the main hall, where he spied his wife alone behind the etched glass panes of the French doors. She was pacing, her posture taut with agitation, her hands nervously working the folds of her gown. He frowned in disapproval, excused himself from the four gentlemen, and moved toward the sitting room.

The Cratchit siblings had gathered in a corner of the banqueting hall. Mary lingered close by, feigning interest in a landscape painting, all the while attuned to their conversation.

"We're all so happy for you, Martha," Belinda said as she embraced her sister warmly. Martha leaned in and whispered, "You're next, Belinda." Belinda replied only with a bashful smile.

"And you!" Martha chided Tim teasingly. "When I have children, are they to see their Uncle Tim with a different woman every time they come to visit?"

"Of course not," said Tim. "By that time, I shall be blissfully married."

Mary smiled silently to herself at Tim's admission.

Then he added: "And all my mistresses will remain safely hidden from your children *and* my wife!"

Tim's siblings laughed, well accustomed to such witty ripostes from their brother. But Mary walked away, not caring to hear any more of the conversation.

"Is there no one special in your life right now, Tim?" Peter asked.

Tim considered his brother's question, then shrugged with a wistful grin. "I don't know. Perhaps. Too soon to tell." He threw his arms in the air and spun full circle on his heels. "But for now, the night is young, and the room is filled with enchanting women who all want to dance with me!"

Tim disappeared into the crowd, grabbing the hand of a young lady. His siblings watched as he twirled her onto the dance floor.

"There was a time when our brother could barely walk," Peter remarked to his siblings. "Now, he's *dancing* at your wedding."

"We all know who we have to thank for that," said Belinda.

Their eyes turned toward Ebenezer Scrooge, who sat at a table, looking gaunt and feeble. He coughed into his kerchief, then sipped from a cup of chamomile tea laced with honey. Martha excused herself and made her way across the room. Despite his frailty, Scrooge's eyes brightened as she approached.

"Uncle Ebenezer," she greeted him warmly.

"Martha, my dear," he said, happy to see her. "How resplendent you look."

She sat beside him, taking his hand in hers. "I heard you weren't feeling well. Do take care of yourself."

"And you, Martha," he said, peering across the room at Thomas. "You take good care of your new husband."

They both looked over at the groom. Ten years Martha's senior, Thomas Stanhope came from a long line of solicitors, barristers, magistrates, and judges—a lineage steeped in contracts and quiet influence. His surname opened doors, and his confidence suggested he'd never encountered one that remained shut. His ability to provide a comfortable life made him a desirable match, if not a particularly romantic one.

"He's a solicitor, I understand," Scrooge said.

Martha smiled. "Yes, but please don't hold that against him." They both chuckled. She kissed him lightly on the cheek. "Bless you, Uncle Ebenezer."

Scrooge smiled. "I *have* been blessed, my dear."

"I have been cursed, my dear," Bob said, "with a low tolerance for alcohol." Now behind closed doors in the sitting room, Bob was in the middle of a heated argument with his wife.

"A poor excuse for showing up drunk at your daughter's wedding!" Abigail responded.

"Perhaps," he argued, "that is because your constant nagging would drive *any* man to drink!"

"You blame everyone but yourself."

"Untrue!" he objected. "I blame *myself* for putting up with your incessant prattle for over thirty years." He grabbed her elbow, guiding her firmly toward the door. "Now come back inside, madam. Standing alone in here, people will talk."

She broke free from his grasp and stood her ground.

"I'm leaving you, Robert."

The silence that followed bristled with defiance, neither willing to yield.

"You'll do no such thing," Bob responded.

"Please believe how difficult this is for me," she said, brushing past him. But Bob seized her wrist, squeezing tightly.

"Why are you doing this?" he demanded. "Do you realize what a scandal this will be? You think a man can keep his standing when his own wife turns her back on him? Are you trying to shame me? Ruin me?"

Abigail did not flinch. She stared at him with a quiet, aching disbelief, as though she no longer recognized the man before her.

"Is that all you care about now? What happens to *you*? What about *your family*?"

Her words landed hard. How could his wife not recognize how he had sacrificed, how he had labored to provide for his family? Everything he did—the business meetings, the long hours, the late nights—it was *all* for them. All of it!

Inside the banqueting hall, Mary stood at the edge of the dance floor, watching Tim glide from one partner to the next. A chill swept over her skin, and she glanced down to see goosebumps rising on her arms, though the room was warm.

"A penny for your thoughts," came a voice at her side. She turned to find Thatch standing uncomfortably close. "Or for you, would it be a *shekel*?"

Mary's jaw tightened. "Good evening, Mr. Thatch," she said, her voice cool and even.

"Good evening, young lady," he replied.

"Young lady," she echoed. "Do you remember the names of "young ladies" in the other firms with which you do business, Mr. Thatch?"

"Of course," he said.

"And yet, you've never bothered to remember mine."

Thatch shrugged. "Names are for people one intends to acknowledge."

Mary steadied herself against the sting of indignity, drawing a long breath and letting it out slowly.

"That young Cratchit is quite the favorite tonight," Thatch continued, nodding toward Tim. "I pity the poor girl who imagines she can tame that colt."

Mary looked across the floor at Tim, who was laughing lightly with two young ladies. She turned to respond—but Thatch had vanished.

Her attention returned to Tim. Her eyes narrowed.

Lifting her skirts, she crossed the floor with quiet purpose, her stride growing bolder with each step.

Reaching Tim's shoulder, she tapped him lightly. He turned to her.

"Good evening, Tim," she said brightly, guiding his right hand to her waist and taking his other hand in hers. "May I claim this dance?"

Startled for a heartbeat, Tim opened his mouth to reply. The French doors to the sitting room suddenly burst open, slamming against the stone walls. All eyes turned toward the sound.

Abigail stood in the threshold, eyes wide and brimming, chest rising with shallow breath. She hesitated for only a moment before she fled forward, her skirts gathering in her hands as she ran—not knowing where she meant to go, only that she must get away. Guests parted in alarm as she passed. Her sobs rising with each step. A hired waiter turned too quickly to avoid her and lost control of his tray, sending china and silverware crashing to the floor. Whether from the tears blurring her vision or the slickness of polished wood beneath her shoes, no one could say, but in the next moment she stumbled, flailed, and fell hard to the ground.

Peter and Tim were at her side instantly, dropping to their knees beside her to help. She did not raise her head. She stared down, weeping, her breathing jagged.

A pair of finely polished black shoes entered her blurred vision, stopping just inches from the hem of her gown. She lifted her head to meet her husband's eyes.

As a server passed, Bob plucked a glass of sparkling wine from the tray and addressed his children, who had all gathered around Abigail.

"Your mother isn't feeling well," he said. "Send for a carriage to take her home."

He nodded to the orchestra, and the music resumed, though the room still buzzed with talk of what had just unfolded.

Turning his back on the family, he emptied his glass in one swallow.

The Ghost's aura shifted to a deep ruby red, and with it came another change in surroundings. Cratchit and the Ghost stood outside Scrooge's townhouse, its austere brick façade rising above the quiet street.

"Not long after your daughter's wedding," the Ghost said, its voice laden with gravity, "you went to visit Scrooge, for the last time."

Cratchit watched as his former self stood at the familiar threshold, glancing at his pocket watch before rapping the heavy knocker against the oak door. It was the same brass knocker where the ghostly face of Jacob Marley had appeared to Scrooge ten years earlier.

The door opened to reveal a gentleman of cheerful aspect, with warm eyes and a ready smile.

"Bob!" he exclaimed, clasping his hand with genuine warmth.

"Good evening, Fred," Bob replied, patting his shoulder with affection.

Scrooge's nephew was still trim and youthful in appearance, with the same open-hearted manner as the first time Bob had met him. For many years, he and Abigail had attended Fred's annual New Year's celebration. Though the invitation still arrived, Bob had begun to usher in the New Year at The Excelsior with his business associates.

"It's so good of you to come." Fred's expression softened, his smile now bittersweet. "He's been asking for you."

The only family that remained to Scrooge was his nephew Fred, yet his house was filled with people. Every seat was taken. Visitors moved somberly through the corridor, their voices hushed. The drawing room and stairwell were lined with acquaintances paying their last respects, speaking in tones no louder than prayer.

Bob gave a brief nod to each guest he passed, following Fred up the stairs and down a quiet corridor, stopping before a closed door. Fred opened the door and gestured Bob inside.

The room beyond was warm and well-appointed. Rich drapes softened the windows, and bookshelves lined the walls, interspersed with framed sketches and scenic oil paintings. Scrooge sat in a wheelchair beside the tall picture window, a knit wrap around his shoulders, a blanket drawn across his knees. His body was fragile, thinned by illness, but his eyes retained their sharpness.

"You're looking well, Ebenezer," Bob said.

"I'm dying, my friend," Scrooge replied, a faint smile on his face. There was no fear in his expression—only a kind of quiet certainty, the look of a man who had come to terms with the sum of his days, and found them, at last, enough.

He turned back to the window. "Look at it, Bob. London in all its splendor."

Bob stepped forward to join him at the window. He saw the glittering rooftops of London silhouetted against the fiery sky. In the distance, the Thames burned orange, catching the final light of the day.

"As the sun sets, the city glimmers like gold," Scrooge murmured. "And yet, most people never even notice." He wheeled himself away from the window. "Because life is full of distractions—isn't it?"

"Yes," Bob said. "Yes, I suppose it is."

The pause in conversation that followed was interminable to Bob. He listened to the old man's heavy, halted breaths; the slow tick of the clock; the winter wind howling through the attic.

"Is there anything you want to tell me, Bob?" Scrooge asked gently.

Bob lowered his gaze, as if searching for the right words.

"There is," he replied. He drew up a chair opposite Scrooge and sat, leaning forward, hands clasped. "Your ledgers. The mistakes you made, the errors we found. I wanted you to know that—" He hesitated.

"Yes?" Scrooge prompted.

Bob looked directly into Ebenezer's eyes and said, "I forgive you."

Scrooge stared back at him, unflinching. "You forgive me," Scrooge repeated, as though he had not heard the words correctly.

"Yes, yes," Bob said evenly. "The company bore the cost of it, but we survived, didn't we? All water under the bridge now. All's forgiven."

Scrooge's expression did not change. He studied Bob with a quiet restraint that belied the gravity of what he was about to say. "I made no mistakes in those ledgers, Bob. My mind is as sharp as ever."

He beckoned Bob closer, slowly leaned in, and whispered in his ear. "I *know* it was you, Bob. What I don't know is—*why*?"

The words struck like a blow. Bob drew back slowly, his breath catching, the world tilting. He had buried that truth so deeply that even hearing it aloud felt unreal. Guilt surfaced for a heartbeat. But contempt surged in, swift and hard, and buried it once more.

"Why?" Bob echoed. He rose and began pacing behind Scrooge's wheelchair. "Why?" he repeated, louder now. "Because I endured your torment for years as a clerk—slaving away, hands frozen in that miserable counting house."

Scrooge angled his wheelchair toward the door, turning to watch him. Bob stopped by the hearth and grabbed a lump of coal from the scuttle.

"'Mr. Cratchit, no more coal! Put it back in the scuttle!'" he sneered, mimicking the Scrooge of old. With a sharp toss, he flung the lump back and kicked the scuttle over, spilling its contents in a shower of coal and black dust.

His eyes landed on a small-framed daguerreotype on the mantel: Scrooge and young Tim, arm in arm. Bob snatched it, holding it aloft.

"Why?" he shouted. "Because you stole my son from me! *My Tim*! You healed his body, but you poisoned his mind. You turned his heart against me. He was mine—not yours! *Mine*!"

In a rage, he hurled the frame against the wall, shattering the glass.

"Why? Why?" he roared, stepping in front of Scrooge's wheelchair.

"So that the company might be rid of you!" he thundered. "I altered the ledgers because you were standing in the firm's way!"

Scrooge lifted his head and met Bob's fury with calm.

"More precisely," Scrooge said quietly, "I was standing in *your* way. Isn't that right?"

Bob didn't reply. The two men simply stared at each other—Scrooge with benevolence, Bob with disdain. Without saying another word, Bob turned to leave, but Scrooge caught his coat sleeve with a gnarled hand.

"Don't worry, my friend," he said. "I'll take your secret to my grave."

Bob looked down at Scrooge's hand and, with studied restraint, removed it from his sleeve.

"Best get on with it, then," Bob replied.

He crossed to the window and yanked the heavy drapes shut. The room fell into near-darkness, lit only by the fire in the hearth and a faint glow that revealed the Ghost and Cratchit standing in the corner. Cratchit stepped forward and stood before the wheelchair, gazing down at Scrooge. Unlike his former self, he felt no anger—only sorrow and remorse for the betrayal. He wished the weight on his heart could be lifted, that his guilt might somehow be absolved.

"Please believe me, Ebenezer, if I could undo what I did to you, I would." Cratchit's voice trembled. He pointed to his former self. "I was blinded by ambition. I was selfish. Spiteful. Ungrateful." Cratchit clasped his hands and fell to his knees in front of Scrooge.

His former self walked stridently to the door and opened it, stopping in the doorway.

"I imagine this will be the last time we see each other, Ebenezer," he said. "*Forgive me* if I don't attend your funeral." Scrooge raised his hand to stop him, but Bob left, slamming the door behind him.

Beneath Scrooge's outstretched hand, Cratchit closed his eyes and bowed his head.

"I'm sorry, Ebenezer," he whispered, sobbing.

"*I forgive you, Bob*," said Scrooge, still staring at the closed door.

Cratchit's breath caught. He lifted his head slowly, just as Scrooge lowered his outstretched arm. For one fragile instant, he believed Scrooge had heard him. Had forgiven him. Then he turned his head to look at the door.

"Spirit," Cratchit said, "were those words meant for my former self—or for me?"

"They were meant for Bob Cratchit," the Spirit replied. "The man you were. The man you are. And the man you've yet to be." The Ghost stepped forward and gestured to Scrooge. "His forgiveness was for then. For now. Forever."

The Ghost's aura grew brighter, bringing warm golden light into the room.

Cratchit wept, and Scrooge's eyes filled with tears as well. Cratchit wished with all his heart that he could remain with his old friend longer—just a few precious moments more—to say a proper goodbye. But the Ghost's aura started to pulse and change color again, signaling this vision was ending. Slowly, quietly, Scrooge and the room around them faded away.

"Ebenezer Scrooge died on Christmas Eve of that year," Cratchit heard the Ghost say.

The street lay cloaked under an ashen sky, mourners packed shoulder to shoulder beneath umbrellas and shawls, all gathered to pay their final respects. A black-draped carriage rolled slowly past, bearing its solemn burden. Sobs rose from the crowd, fragile and scattered. Men doffed their hats, women crossed themselves, and children threw flowers onto the wet cobblestones in front of the hearse.

"While the rest of London mourned his passing," the Ghost continued, "I wonder, did you feel any compassion in your heart, Robert?"

Inside the offices of Scrooge and Cratchit, Bob stood in his waistcoat and shirtsleeves, unmoving, his face stony as he watched from behind the front picture window. The funeral procession filed past in mournful silence, black umbrellas bobbing beneath the steady rain.

Outside, a ladder leaned against the building's façade. A worker, soaked to the skin, wrestled with the rain-swollen sign above the entrance. With some effort, the nameboard bearing 'Scrooge & Cratchit' was taken down. Bob's eyes shifted from the procession to the new sign being hoisted into place: 'Cratchit & Sons'. A faint smile tugged at the corner of his lips.

From the rain-slicked pavement, Cratchit stood outside the window, face to face with the man he had once been. As dusk folded swiftly into night, he saw the image of his former self grow dimmer, until the figure vanished entirely, leaving only Cratchit's reflection in the glass staring back at him.

The street lay empty. The mourners had vanished, the horses gone, the silence returned. A bitter wind howled down the deserted road, curling through the iron railings and tugging at the shutters of darkened shops. Loose papers chased one another in frenzied flight, skittering along the cobblestones.

“Spirit?” Cratchit called into the gloom, suddenly feeling weary and quite alone. “Where are you—?”

No reply came from the empty street—only the moan of wind and the distant tolling of a bell striking the hour.

STAVE THREE

Secrets of the Present

Through the picture window, Cratchit saw a flame leap to life inside the building. His eyes flew open in alarm. "Fire! Fire!" he cried.

Without pause, he burst through the door and seized the wooden bucket of water kept by the entrance—a prudent precaution in any London premises since the days of the Great Fire. Intent on dousing the blaze, he didn't notice the figure standing just inside, torch in hand.

The Ghost greeted him joyfully. "Merry—"

"Fire!" Cratchit shouted, throwing the water at him.

"—Christmas," the Spirit finished, not quite so merry. He was soaked from his auburn hair to his gold-buckled boots. The Ghost looked from his smoldering torch to Cratchit, who sheepishly tried to hide the empty bucket behind his back.

"I'm—I'm sorry," Cratchit stammered. "I didn't mean to—"

The Ghost burst into laughter—a deep, rolling roar that echoed off the rafters and filled the room with warmth. "No harm done," he said, giving Cratchit a hearty slap on the back. "We won't let a little water dampen our spirits, eh?"

With a grand sweep of his hand over the soaked torch, it blazed anew. At once, his garments dried, his curls sprang back into place, and the glow returned to his round and ruddy cheeks. He gave the torch a dramatic whirl above his head, and the entire room lit up, revealing a sight to behold.

Wreaths adorned the doors. A towering Christmas tree glittered in one corner, its branches heavy with ornaments and tinsel. Great swags of garland draped the mantel and rafters. Tables groaned beneath roast game, steaming puddings, candied fruits, and flagons of mulled wine. Gaily wrapped parcels spilled across the floor, stacked high as the ceiling.

"Come closer," the Spirit urged, beckoning with a broad hand. "Don't you recognize me?"

Cratchit shook his head in response as he slowly approached.

"You knew my brothers," said the Ghost, his voice rich as brandy. "Years ago, you kept Christmas as well as any man alive."

The words rekindled a warmth in him—distant, but unmistakable.

"I am the Ghost of Christmas Present," the Spirit declared.

"But how am I to know you if we've never met?" Cratchit's eyes drifted from the Spirit to the feast laid before him.

The Spirit smiled. "You have but to look. I am with the children who sing carols beneath the lamplight. I am beside the poor in workhouses and hospitals. I visit humble dwellings and noble houses alike. Wherever there is kindness, generosity, and fellowship—there you will find me."

While the Spirit spoke, Cratchit helped himself to a piece of mincemeat pie, which he bit into with great enthusiasm.

"Don't stop," he said, his speech garbled by a mouthful of pie. "Pray, tell me more."

"Touch my robe, Bob Cratchit," said the Spirit. "We have little time."

"Not just yet, Spirit," Cratchit said, eyeing a ham glistening with honeyed glaze. "I have much to eat—" he caught himself. "To learn."

The Spirit observed Cratchit's focus on the feast, and cautioned, "You do know gluttony is one of the seven deadly sins."

Cratchit cast a sly glance at the Spirit's expansive belly. "That's a bit like the pot calling the kettle black, wouldn't you say?"

The Ghost looked down at his considerable girth and erupted into laughter once again—a sound so full and merry it sent the garlands rustling and the candle flames swaying. Cratchit joined in, biting into a turkey leg and wishing that all spirits were as hospitable as this one. If that were so, then he would welcome a visitation any day of the year!

Still laughing, the Ghost threw a massive arm around Cratchit's shoulder, and in good fellowship, Cratchit did the same, his hand brushing the Spirit's robe.

In an instant, the entire scene vanished, and they were no longer in the company building. They stood in the parlor room of Cratchit's own home, bathed in gentle morning light. The air was filled with the warm scent of pine and spice, and a fire crackled in the hearth.

"Observe one who still keeps Christmas in her heart," said the Ghost with quiet reverence. "Your daughter."

Cratchit's gaze turned to the figure by the mantel. "Belinda—" he whispered.

She stood modest and graceful in a dark green gown, bending gently over a box wrapped in brown paper. At her feet, the eager terrier waited, tail wagging furiously.

"Merry Christmas, Chester," she said softly. "I have a present for you."

She opened the parcel with the blade of a pair of scissors. "Brand new slippers for you to chew on," she announced, placing them on the floor, "so that Father's slippers might remain in one piece." Chester gave an enthusiastic yap and immediately seized one of the slippers between his teeth, gnawing contentedly.

A warm voice echoed from the doorway. "Merry Christmas, my love!"

Belinda turned. "Randall!" she exclaimed, running into his arms and wrapping him in a passionate embrace.

"Have you been a good boy this year?" she teased, walking with him to the hearth.

"I have been exceedingly good," Randall replied with mock formality.

"In that case," she said, lifting another parcel from the mantel, "I have something for you." The little dog barked again, anticipating another gift. "They're not *all* for you, Chester," she said, laughing. As they both sat on the sofa, she handed the gift to Randall. "Merry Christmas, darling."

He peeled back the paper and opened the box to reveal a pocket watch, and a quite handsome one at that. She prompted him to click open the watch's hunter-case cover, which he did.

"What does it say?" she asked excitedly.

"Why, it says half past eleven," Randall replied.

"Not the time, silly goose. The inscription!"

He read aloud what was etched on the back cover. *"Randall, I shall love you now and forever, till the end of time—Belinda."* Looking up at her, he said, "It's beautiful. As beautiful as you."

They kissed. And as they pulled apart, Randall took a moment to study her face with quiet affection. "My turn," he said, withdrawing an envelope from his inside coat pocket, and holding it up for her to see.

"This is a letter to my father. It states emphatically that I will *not* be marrying a bride he chose for me. Because *I've* already chosen my bride."

Randall reached into his coat and drew out a small white box. As he lifted the lid, Belinda's eyes widened at the sight within. There, nestled in a bed of velvet, was a small diamond ring. Her breath caught. She looked from the ring to Randall, her lips parting in surprise.

"It isn't much," he said earnestly, watching her closely. "But it's what I could afford on a clerk's wages."

Dropping to one knee, he gazed up at her with unguarded devotion. "Belinda Cratchit—will you do me the honor of becoming my wife?" She held her breath as he carefully slipped the ring onto her finger. She looked down at the ring, the firelight catching its facets, and for a moment, the world around her seemed to vanish. Her face softened with wonder, overwhelmed by the promise held in that simple ring.

A slipper clutched in his mouth, Chester hopped onto a chair by the fireplace and knocked Bob's hat to the floor. She glanced at the hat, and her joy faded. A sudden realization replaced happiness with hesitation. The corners of her mouth quivered. She rose from the couch and stepped away.

"I don't know what to say."

"Say yes," he replied, rising from his knee and stepping over to her. "Say yes, and I'll ask your father for your hand this very day."

Belinda stared at the ring, her body trembling. She had to choose between love and loyalty. Randall wanted her, her father needed her. She looked over at Bob's hat where it lay beside the hearth. Slowly, she bent to retrieve it, her fingers tightening around the brim. For a moment, she simply held it—silent, still—looking from the hat to the ring. Then slowly, painfully, she slipped the gold band from her finger and returned it to Randall.

His face fell, and he struggled to speak. "I don't understand. Is it because of my position?"

"No, of course not," she said quickly.

Randall hesitated. "Is it because I'm—"

"Never!" she replied before the words could escape his lips.

"Then—why?" he asked.

She turned away from him. "Because he needs me."

Randall hesitated for a moment, but then spoke freely. "Yes, he needs you. To clean up his messes. To make excuses to others for his behavior."

"My father is a good man," she insisted.

"You know how much he drinks—"

"A *good* man," she repeated.

"How much money he squanders gambling—"

"Stop it, Randall," she cautioned.

"—what company he keeps until the small hours of the morning—"

"Stop it!" she shouted, turning to him.

"He's a broken man, Belinda. *And you—cannot—fix him.*"

He held out the envelope, his voice rising. "I'm standing up to *my* father! I'm giving up my inheritance—my position with his firm—for you. *For us!* Why can *you* not do the same?"

"Because it's *not* the same," she insisted. "Your father doesn't love *you*."

"And yours thinks only of himself!" He snatched the hat from her hand and threw it across the room. Cratchit watched as it passed cleanly through the Ghost, hitting the wall behind them.

Belinda's tone shifted from defiance to anger. "Why don't you just say it? You *hate* my father!"

"No," Randall said, his voice quieter. "But I hate what he's doing to *you*. And I hate what you've done to *yourself*."

He stepped forward and grabbed her hand. She tried to pull away, but he held fast. Gently, he rolled up her sleeve. The soft light revealed faint lines along her forearm. Some older, faded to pale silver; others more recent, barely healed. Her skin bore quiet testimony to unspoken pain.

Cratchit gasped. Randall's eyes shifted to the scissors resting on the end table, then back to her.

"You said you stopped."

"I—I tried," she whispered. "It's getting better."

"It's getting worse," he said.

He reached for her other arm and quickly pulled up the sleeve. More lines revealed themselves, one after another. Some were alone, others crisscrossing. Each cut a reminder of the despair she'd borne in silence.

She could have begged for Randall's understanding and forgiveness. She could have accused him of forcing her to make an impossible choice. She could have lied, saying she had a momentary lapse but that now everything was under control.

Instead, she looked into his eyes and said, "Promise you won't tell Father."

Randall stood there for a long moment, helpless, and for the first time—hopeless. Slowly, he let go of her hand. Belinda brushed past him and collapsed onto the sofa, tears streaming down her face as she rolled down her sleeves.

Randall observed her with sadness and pity. Not knowing what else he could say or do, he simply retrieved his hat and opened the front door. Their eyes met—his filled with ache, hers with apology. Then, silently, he bowed his head (not in formality, but in surrender) and stepped into the cold.

Cratchit and the Ghost watched in silence. "Your daughter's love for you is so great," the Spirit observed, "that she would sacrifice her own happiness for your sake."

The little terrier tugged at the chain of Randall's pocket watch where it rested on the table, pulling it onto the stone hearth and shattering the crystal face.

Randall emerged from the front door of the Cratchit house just as Peter and his young family were mounting the steps.

"Ah, Mr. Yates. A Merry Christmas!" Peter greeted him warmly. Randall touched the brim of his hat with stiff politeness. "Mr. Cratchit. Mrs. Cratchit," he acknowledged, his eyes not quite meeting theirs as he passed them on the steps.

"Not staying for Christmas dinner?" Peter asked, confused.

"A sudden change of plans, I'm afraid," Randall replied curtly as he reached the bottom of the steps.

Peter called after him with a sense of some urgency, "A moment of your time, sir!"

Randall stopped, resting his gloved hand on the black iron railing. Peter turned to his wife, his tone gentle. "I'll join you shortly, darling." He kissed her cheek and tousled his son's hair affectionately. Randall watched them with the stony air of a man longing for a dream he'd been denied. The boy and his mother continued up the steps, as Peter descended to meet with Randall.

Peter's voice lowered, speaking confidentially, one man to another. "Yesterday at the office—Mr. Hobbs' comments about my father's drinking were completely inappropriate—and damaging to the company, should rumors circulate."

Randall gave a solemn nod. "I understand," he said and turned to leave, but Peter grabbed his elbow.

"Also," he added carefully, "Mr. Hobbs' suggestion that I take over the company—"

"Oh, but it's true, Peter," Randall interrupted with unexpected gravitas. "You *should* consider it, and quickly. For everything your father touches—*he destroys*."

Peter stared at him, eyes narrowed, surprised by his bluntness. Randall cast a final glance up at the house before taking his leave, yesterday's snowfall crunching beneath his shoes. Peter watched him walk away with a look that questioned what had transpired just before his arrival.

Randall passed by the Ghost and Cratchit on the pavement, not aware of their presence. Cratchit looked up at the house to see Belinda standing in the window, her hand gently touching the glass pane.

With the wave of the Spirit's torch, the scene transformed to the countryside estate of Martha and Thomas Stanhope, which stood serene beneath a pale and cloud-streaked Christmas sky. The stone manor was a fine property, dignified without being ostentatious, and enviably situated just beyond the bustle of London's smoky confines.

Such comforts had not arrived by fortune's whim, but by industry and perseverance: Thomas, a solicitor of sharp intellect and sharper tongue, had built his reputation on contracts no loophole could slip through, while Martha, with quiet ambition and impeccable taste, operated a modest but thriving millinery in the City.

Their household, though prosperous, was not without shadows. No children played in the hedgerows or trundled hoops across the gravel drive, and it seemed none ever would. An illness shortly after their marriage had taken its toll on Martha. Her health had since returned, but the hope of bearing a child had not.

On the porch of the estate, Abigail Cratchit sat wrapped in a shawl, her knitting needles moving with slow, meditative purpose. Her cheeks held the fragile bloom of a woman who bore her sorrows with grace.

"Your wife Abigail's love, like your daughter's, goes unanswered," the Spirit said.

Cratchit bristled. "Have I made her life so miserable, Spirit? Have I not provided for my wife? Showered her with expensive garments and jewelry?"

"You have given her fine gifts," the Spirit agreed. "But you have deprived her of *that which she needs most* from you. If these shadows remain unaltered by the future—"

The Spirit pointed to Abigail.

"—your wife will not see another Christmas. She will die of a broken heart."

From the doorway of the house, Martha stepped lightly onto the porch's wooden planks, a wrap of beige lace draped over her shoulders. Her mother looked up from her knitting with a sad smile, unable to mask the sorrow of being estranged from her husband and not living in her own home.

Martha eased herself into the wicker chair beside her, and together they sat, the rhythm of the needles clicking like a metronome to the easy cadences of their conversation. They spoke of trifles at first. How red the holly berries looked in church that morning. How the minister's booming voice had quaked with conviction during the sermon. How the choir had sung so sweetly that it brought tears to Abigail's eyes. They laughed about Widow

Culpepper's latest scandal. They wondered whether Randall would someday propose to their beloved Belinda. They mused over Peter's soon-to-be-born child. Abigail suspected it would be a boy, Martha a girl. Both smiled at the thought of another small hand to hold.

There were moments of silence, too, filled not with awkwardness, but with the kind of ease that comes from years of shared burdens and joys. Abigail touched Martha's hand, her eyes misting with a tenderness too deep for words. Martha squeezed it back, and in that simple act was the whole history of their bond.

Something in Cratchit's chest tightened as he beheld the intimacy between his wife and daughter, so effortless and deep-rooted. It wasn't the ache of sentiment. No, it was something sharper, more shameful.

It was envy. Envy of the bond they shared—so easy, so natural. He wanted that closeness, yearned for it. But he now realized that such bonds were not gifted by blood alone; they were earned by presence, by care, by time.

His thoughts drifted to Belinda, and to the pain she must be feeling. Seeing the scars on her arms had shocked him. How had he missed her silent cries for help? He remembered her downcast eyes yesterday morning. He struggled to recall what they had talked about. Ah yes, she had asked for the first dance of the evening. And he had promised it to her—only to forget her request, lost in the whirl of his own concerns and pleasures.

Now he wondered how many promises he had broken, how many moments he had overlooked while she waited for the warmth of a glance, a kind word, a father's gentle praise. For what child, young or grown, should ever have to guess at a father's love?

The door behind the two women opened, and Thomas stepped onto the porch. He cast a glance at his wife—a subtle inquiry, silent but clear. Martha met his eyes and gave the smallest of nods before turning to stoop gently beside her mother's chair.

"Mother, Thomas and I have been talking," she said. "Shall we go for a walk?"

The park was hushed beneath a blanket of overcast skies, the air crisp with the scent of damp earth. A gravel path wound its way past neatly trimmed hedges and trellises, where a few hardy winter blooms still clung to life. Abigail moved slowly, each step measured, her arm resting lightly on her daughter's.

Cratchit and the Spirit followed a few steps behind.

Abigail nodded politely at a passing matron, then turned to Martha with the wistful look of someone conjuring up a distant past.

"How our lives have changed since you were a child, Martha. When we had no money, I would pass ladies of society and, God forgive me, I'd be jealous. As I sewed the holes in my twice-turned gowns, I thought, *"If only I had their satins, their lace."* Now that I have those things, all I want is my old life back—in our little house. That cold, damp, *wonderful* little house."

Thomas walked quietly beside them, then spoke with uncommon directness. "Your lives have changed because your *husband* has changed, hasn't he?"

Mrs. Cratchit gave a sorrowful nod, the wool of her shawl bunched tightly in her hands. "He's no longer the man I married."

Cratchit's jaw clenched. "The man she married was weak and naive," he explained to the Spirit. "He was a simpleton. *A pawn.*"

"A pawn—who now aspires to be a *Knight*," the Ghost said wryly.

"And what's wrong with that?" Cratchit countered. "Becoming a Knight Paragon is a noble goal."

"Yes," answered the Spirit. "And exactly how many brandies and cigars does it take for one to achieve this goal?"

The pale morning sun dimmed behind a blanket of thick, sunless cloud. A distant rumble of thunder rolled across the hills.

"Mrs. Cratchit, if I may be blunt," Thomas continued, clearing his throat, "should you and your husband part ways, I'd be willing to help ensure your interests are protected and your affairs properly managed."

Cratchit's fists curled at his sides. "Aha!" he exclaimed. "Now I see my son-in-law's true intent. He wants control of *my money*!"

The Spirit offered no rebuke, only a reasoned observation. "It's time *someone* exercised control over your money, wouldn't you agree?"

Thunder again, closer now, and louder. Rain began to fall in tentative droplets, scattering dark coins upon the garden path. A street vendor in the distance hastened to close his awning. They walked toward the park's covered gazebo.

“Perhaps,” Abigail said wearily, “we should talk about this some other time.”

“Time is running short, madam,” Thomas said, his cadence shifting. He sounded like a man accustomed to presenting arguments before magistrates. “Look at what your household has been exposed to. Inebriation. Debauchery. Immorality.”

“How much longer must I listen, Spirit?” Cratchit muttered under his breath. “Life’s too short for long speeches.”

“So you’ve said,” chuckled the Ghost.

“Tim still lives under your husband’s roof,” Thomas resumed. “You can see the damage it’s doing to him.”

“It’s true,” Mrs. Cratchit agreed sadly. “The innocence I once saw in Tim is gone.”

Martha put an arm around her mother and gently helped her into the gazebo, its broad white beams sheltering a few garden benches from the growing drizzle. Around them, other guests huddled beneath parasols or darted inside to take refuge from the rain.

Once Abigail and Martha had settled onto a bench, Thomas continued. “Your husband cares only for himself.”

Abigail wavered. Her shoulders sagged. “I can’t think. I’m very tired.”

“He has failed as a husband, *and* as a father,” Thomas said sharply, each phrase now landing with the finality of a closing argument.

“That’s enough for now, Thomas,” Martha interjected, sensing that her husband was pressing too hard. Abigail closed her eyes, her lips quivering slightly. “I want to go home.”

"Mother, it's raining. We'll be drenched."

"I want to go home," Abigail insisted.

"You *have* no home, madam."

"Thomas!" Martha admonished, but he did not stop.

"Your husband has taken your happiness. Your health. *And* your home."

With a deafening crash of thunder, the heavens broke open, unleashing a torrent of rain. Tears flowing down her cheeks, Abigail fell into Martha's arms, her sobs swallowed by the downpour.

Though the rain fell around Cratchit and the Spirit, the flame of the torch was unaffected, and they didn't feel the chill of the rain on their skin, for these were mere shadows to which they bore witness. As they began to walk, the rain ceased, and the setting changed to the streets of London Town. It was almost dusk.

Cratchit turned to the Spirit, eyes filled with sorrow. His voice came raw and hoarse. "Is it true, Spirit? Have I failed my wife and children?"

They passed by a muddy alleyway, not noticing the soldier there, braced against the wall. He was rolling up his sleeve, a small tin of morphine in one hand, a syringe in the other.

"I look at Peter and see an exceptional young man," Cratchit said.

Just before he prepared to insert the needle into his arm, the soldier raised his head to see Peter staring at him.

"Successful. Well-adjusted. Strong-willed," Cratchit continued. The soldier slowly extended his arm and offered the syringe to Peter, who stared at it.

"And Tim," Cratchit mused. "One day he'll be a fine businessman. Follow in his father's footsteps."

"Indeed, Robert," the Ghost replied. "He *is* following in your footsteps."

They stopped in front of The Lion's Head Pub and looked in its cracked glass window. Amidst the weathered patrons sat Tim, shoulders hunched and breath fogging the rim of his empty tankard.

He rose, swaying slightly. From behind the bar, the publican called out, voice thick with suspicion. "'Ere now, where you off to without settlin' your bill?"

Tim turned with mock grandeur, planting one hand on the table for balance. "Good sir, I shall come into a tidy sum tomorrow, at which time I will pay you and celebrate with all my—"

He motioned with a sweep of his arm to the motley group of pub patrons.

"—good friends. Until then, good day."

With exaggerated gallantry, Tim straightened his rumpled shirt and staggered out the door. Behind him, the barkeep snorted. "Cock and bull."

The street outside was damp and greasy from the earlier rain, and fresh snow was beginning to fall. Chimney smoke curled above, but down here the cold slid into the bones. Tim rounded a corner, heading home, when his eyes landed on two shadowy figures conversing across the way by the names of Darby and Stokes.

Although Mr. Darby fancied himself a self-taught scholar, he was unaccustomed to pondering thoughts more complex than what to consume for midday dinner. His long overcoat bulged with dog-eared pamphlets and pilfered volumes of poetry and plays. Mr. Stokes spoke less than Mr. Darby, but what he lacked in brains, he made up for in brawn. They leaned against a lamp post, looking for their next mark.

Upon seeing the men, Tim quickly turned on his heels. But it was too late. They'd seen Tim.

"Oi, Cratchit!" yelled Darby, flicking away his cigarette. The two men began chasing after him.

Tim broke into a sprint, bursting back into the pub, upending chairs and muttering apologies to the pub patrons, who seemed unbothered and uninterested. His boots skidded on spilled ale as he vaulted over the bar. Behind the counter, the barkeep howled in protest as a tin tray of spoons clattered to the floor.

Through the swinging kitchen doors he went, the smell of boiling mutton and burnt onions hitting him in the face. The cook and pot boy looked up in surprise as Tim slid across the length of the slick kitchen floor, before bursting through the back exit.

The alley beyond was lined with overflowing ash bins. Rats scattered as he ran, the hem of his coat catching on broken crates and puddles rippling under his footfalls. Darby and Stokes were not far behind.

He spotted a red door at the rear of a nearby building, threw it open, and staggered into a hallway suffused with rose-scented powder and cheap perfume. He ran up a stairway. Silken drapes parted as he barreled down a corridor lit by flickering sconces.

Bursting into a parlor, he was confronted with a half-dozen women in various stages of undress. Rouge-stained lips parted in surprise. He had stumbled into a brothel.

Chest heaving, he blinked at the ladies as they stared back. A madam of commanding presence and generous curves stepped in front of him.

"You are without a doubt the most *eager* customer we've *ever* had!" she quipped.

Behind him, Tim heard boots thundering up the steps. He spun and ran down the brothel's adjacent hallway, flung open a side door, and ducked into a dimly lit bedchamber.

A half-naked gentleman and a working girl gasped and sat up in bed as Tim burst in.

"Excuse me, miss," he apologized to the woman. "Constable," he said, addressing the man beside her. He darted to the far wall, opened the window, and scrambled out like a cat fleeing a rooftop fire.

Moments later, Darby and Stokes barreled into the room. The man and woman in bed both pointed silently to the now-swinging windowpane.

Tim landed in the back of a hay cart, vanishing in a puff of straw before tumbling off the side as the startled driver shouted curses. Darting down the nearest avenue, he slipped between stalls selling parsnips and pickled eels, then hurdled a rag-and-bone man dozing beside a barrel fire.

Turning a corner, he ran directly into Stokes, a wall of sheer muscle and beer breath. "Fancy meeting you here, Mr. Cratchit," he rumbled, catching Tim by the shirt.

Darby appeared seconds later, out of breath. Tim acted glad to see them, as his eyes darted for an escape route.

"Good afternoon, gentlemen!" he said cheerfully.

"Not for you, it ain't," Darby growled.

Cratchit and the Ghost watched the men drag Tim into a narrow alley. Cratchit's voice was filled with dread. "Spirit, you must do something to help."

"We can only observe," came the reply.

"But—it's my son!"

A huge fist slammed into Tim's face, his head snapping back against the soot-slick bricks with a sickening crack. Blood oozed from a split lip. Stokes pinned him by the throat, his fingers grinding against Tim's windpipe.

"Not so fast, Mr. Stokes. Perhaps Cratchit has the money he owes us," Darby said, his voice lilting with mockery.

"Not bleedin' likely," Stokes muttered.

Darby turned to a heap of rubbish near the wall and plucked from it the leg of a shattered Windsor chair, still bearing a jagged edge and a rusted nail. He gave it a few practice swings, then tapped it rhythmically against his open palm. "Cratchit, you're a gambling man. How many bones do you suppose I could break with one whack of this lovely club?" he mused.

Tim's breath rasped in his throat. "A few more days. I assure you—" He never finished. Stokes' fist slammed into his stomach, lifting him from the ground. Tim collapsed to his knees with a dry heave, his arms wrapped around his ribs.

"If it wouldn't be *too* inconvenient, we'd like our money *now*, Cratchit," Darby said, crouching beside him.

"And you'll get it. Tomorrow, I swear!" Tim gasped, struggling for air.

Darby smashed the club into the bricks beside Tim's ear. Bits of mortar exploded outward. "Tomorrow, and tomorrow, and tomorrow," he intoned with theatrical relish. "Shakespeare. Macbeth. A tragic figure, Mr. Stokes." He grabbed Tim by the hair, forcing his bruised face upward. "Not unlike our young friend here."

Through swollen eyes, Tim looked up to see a light in a room across the alley. Behind the window, a man's face appeared, a witness to the beating. The man's gaze lingered only a moment, before he reached up and drew the curtains shut.

Darby savagely pulled Tim up by his hair. "Have you ever had crutches before, Mr. Cratchit?" Darby asked. "You'll be needing them, I'm afraid." He passed the club to Stokes.

"Break his legs," Darby ordered.

Tim's eyes went wide. "Noooo!"

The club came down like a hammer against his legs. He screamed in agony, collapsing to his knees. Writhing in the filth, he clawed at the stones, gasping for breath.

Stokes raised the club again—

"Stop!" came a cry from the entrance to the alley. Both men turned.

There at the far opening stood Mary, framed by the narrowing walls and swirling snow.

"Let him go," she insisted, stepping forward.

"Not bleedin' likely," Stokes replied. "He's a hard one to catch."

"Walk away, miss. You want no part of this," Darby said. But she kept advancing, joining the three men in the filthy alley. Her voice remained commanding, eyes steady with resolve, but her hands quivered slightly at her sides.

"Let me pose a question to you, gentlemen. Would you rather have your debt repaid—or your debtor disabled?" she asked.

Darby paused, as if giving her question serious thought.

"I like the sound of both," he said at last, turning to Stokes. "You?"

Stokes grinned and nodded.

Darby turned back to Mary with mock courtesy. "Both, miss. Debt repaid, debtor disabled. And in that order, if you please."

The two men threw their heads back, howling. Darby barely choked out his next words through the laughter.

"Give 'im another whack, Mr. Stokes—if you please."

But as the club lifted once more, Mary stepped forward, placing herself between the men and Tim.

"I have something you might want," she said.

Darby's eyes looked her over with brazen interest, his mouth curving into a lewd grin. "Well, now. What is it you have for us, miss?"

Mary reached beneath her coat and drew out her gold chain with the locket at the end, holding it out for Darby.

"Mary, don't give—" Tim began, his voice weak. Stokes cut him off with an elbow to his face. "You've got nothing to say in the matter."

Darby plucked the necklace from Mary's delicate fingers with his grimy hand. He flipped open the locket and didn't notice the four-leaf clover fall out and flutter to the snowy ground.

"This is your lucky day, Cratchit. You'd be a cripple right now if it weren't for this little lady," Darby said, tucking the necklace into his coat pocket. "We'll be back tomorrow for the rest."

Stokes dropped the club. It landed beside Tim near a crimson splatter in the snow.

"A pleasure doing business with you, miss," Darby said, flashing a grin as vile as the alley stench. The two men sauntered past her, letting their eyes linger, laughing as they walked off.

Mary rushed to Tim's side, kneeling in the snow, her hands cradling his battered face. "You're hurt," she said softly.

"I'm fine," Tim insisted, though pain twisted every word. "But how did you—"

"I saw you being chased," she said simply. "I followed."

Tim tried to sit up. Mary slipped an arm around his back and helped him. The snow was falling harder now.

"Your necklace—"

"It's not important," she said.

"It was your mother's. I'll get it back—"

"You mustn't!" she cut him off, raising her voice. "Can't you see how much more you mean than some silly old necklace?"

Tim closed his eyes, his breathing shallow and faltering. He succumbed to his body's exhaustion, slowly tilting his head forward to rest his forehead against hers.

"I heard somewhere," she whispered, "that this is how the Maori in New Zealand greet each other."

They felt each other's warm breath against their lips and cheeks.

"I rather like it," he replied. He pulled his head back and looked into her face, as if seeing it for the first time—

studying every line, every shadow. Lifting his hand, he gently brushed his fingertips across her cheek, leaving three faint trails of his blood on her skin.

"Those men were right," he said. "You should have walked away."

Pressing the weight of his body against the wall, he winced at the sharp pain in his ribs as he stood. Without another word, he began to limp away, clenching his teeth with each excruciating step.

Mary stood and watched him walk away.

"You love me!" she shouted after him.

He stopped, straightening slightly as her words rang out.

"If not now, you will, Tim Cratchit!"

Slowly, Tim turned back to her, bruised and bloodied, one hand braced against the brick wall to steady himself.

"If that's true, Mary—"

He paused. She stood resolute, her chest rising and falling as her breathing quickened.

"—then heaven help us both," he said finally.

Mary's breath caught as his words took hold. Her eyes began to glisten, and she smiled at him, raising her chin just a bit higher. He slowly broke into a smile of his own—that boyish grin that had attracted her from the day they first met.

And for a moment in time, they remained facing each other, silent, like two statues in the snow.

Cratchit's voice broke the stillness. "Is this the crowd my son runs with, Spirit? Rogues and scoundrels?"

The Ghost answered with grave clarity. "A sorry lot, yes. But are they really any different from *your* acquaintances, Robert?"

With a wave of the Spirit's torch, Cratchit found himself in another familiar setting—the dark-paneled study of The Excelsior. The ornate gold clock on the wall loomed large. Its gilded hands crept toward midnight with ceremonial slowness.

"Just three more minutes till Christmas Day, gentlemen," noted Ramsey. Hawkins and Quill gathered around a serving trolley, while Thatch sat in a plush leather chair by the fire, sipping a dark cocktail that resembled black ink.

Hawkins sighed. "Ah, Christmas. The blessed Day of Revaluation."

Ramsey chuckled in agreement. "It's beautiful watching loan rates rise just as the snow begins to fall."

"This year, no less than six company presidents we do business with will find coal in their stockings."

"Socializing with all of them has been insufferable. Especially—*him*!" Ramsey said.

"Riff-raff!" Quill joined in, then asked quietly, "Whom are we talking about?"

"Cratchit," Ramsey and Hawkins said in unison.

"Do you suppose he suspects?" Quill asked.

"You give the man far too much credit," Hawkins replied, smirking. "Cratchit's nothing more than a glorified clerk."

Thatch rose and lit a cigar with theatrical flair as he approached the others.

"Quite true," he agreed. "The man *is* out of his depth. But the *reason* he doesn't realize what tragedy awaits him is because—"

He exhaled a slow stream of smoke and smiled.

"—he trusts us. We are his *friends*."

The men chuckled, as Quill raised his glass. “To Mr. Thatch.”

Thatch waved the toast away. “No, no, gentlemen. To Bob Cratchit! To his foolish dream of rising above his station—and his misguided faith in the better nature of Man. We are all the richer for his delusions.”

The men began to laugh, the sound deep and self-satisfied. Gradually it grew louder, until the room resounded with their laughter.

Cratchit watched from the shadows, blood pounding in his ears. “Rotters!” he shouted at them. “You’re out to ruin me! I thought you were men of your word, but Peter was right. You are liars and thieves, the whole lot of you!”

The men’s laughter swelled, grotesque and echoing, bouncing off the marble columns and mahogany walls. The hands of the clock clicked into place and began to strike midnight.

“Stop this! I demand it! I will not be made a fool of!” Cratchit shouted.

Yet the laughter continued unabated, merging with the clanging of the clock. The strikes grew louder, harsher, a deafening, hellish din.

The Ghost of Christmas Present faded away as Cratchit covered his ears. “Stop it!” he cried, staggering backwards. “Stop the laughing! Stop the clanging! Enough!”

Cratchit turned and fled the club, running into the street, heedless of where he went. The clock tower’s bell striking the hour added its own loud, dissonant clanging to the din.

Snow swirled about Cratchit as he raced through the streets of St. James to escape the growing cacophony. But no matter how far away he ran, the noise only grew louder.

As he staggered into a crossroads, a jolt of fear stopped him in his tracks.

Bearing down on him with terrifying speed came four monstrous black horses, their hooves pounding the stones, eyes burning red. The clanging and the laughter rang louder in his ears as the horses surged forward, their spectral forms looming larger with every stride. Cratchit raised his hands as he braced for impact—

—and they passed through him.

The sensation was like falling into icy water: a jolt of cold so deep it left no breath behind. Cratchit stumbled, but did not fall. He stood still, gasping, welcoming the sudden silence.

Then, sensing a presence so powerful it pressed in on the senses, he slowly turned.

A great black hearse stood motionless in the street behind him, its frame draped in velvet and iron, wheels glistening with frost. The horses that pulled it now stood still, their hooves pawing the cobblestones, breath rising from their nostrils in great steaming clouds.

Above them, on the driver's bench, a skeletal hand unclenched from the reins and withdrew into the folds of a heavy black cloak.

Stave Four

Visions of the Future

The Phantom stepped down from the cab. As the hem of its robe touched the ground, the horses and hearse dissolved into mist.

The Ghost loomed, tall and still, draped and hooded in a black garment that swallowed the light. No face, no voice, no form was visible beneath the folds of darkness.

"Can you speak, Spirit?" Cratchit asked, his voice quavering. "Or is it that you have no words of hope to give me?"

The Phantom did not move and did not respond. Cratchit stepped closer to the Spirit.

"Are you the Ghost of Christmas Yet to Come?" he asked.

The Phantom raised a skeletal hand, finger outstretched. Cratchit looked at it quizzically, as though enduring a game of charades with an especially unhelpful partner.

"You want me to take your hand, is that it?" Cratchit asked. The Ghost didn't answer.

"Very well, Spirit."

He grasped the Phantom's finger—only for it to snap off in his grip. Cratchit flinched at the sound, then looked down at the bony finger in his palm.

“Perhaps you didn’t want me to take your hand,” he said meekly, with an apologetic smile. He quickly tried reattaching the Spirit’s finger, but it fell to the ground. As he kneeled to retrieve it, the bone dissolved to dust and blew away in the wind.

Hearing an odd clicking sound above his head, Cratchit looked up. The Phantom’s outstretched hand was transforming—bone and cartilage regenerating to replace the missing finger. With small pops and crackles, it grew with unnatural speed—joint by joint—until the full finger was restored.

As Cratchit stood, he realized they were now in front of his place of business. The Spirit flexed its new appendage, then turned and pointed.

“You wish me to enter, Spirit?” Cratchit asked. The Phantom nodded.

As they approached the building, Cratchit noticed that the ornate copper door had been replaced with plain oak. He reached for the handle, but the door swung open on its own by unseen hands. With the Phantom close behind, he cautiously stepped inside. The sight that greeted him was both shocking and heartbreaking.

The space had changed in every particular. It now bore the stripped-down look of an office being dismantled. Desks and furnishings were pared to the bone. The chandeliers had been sold off, the marble fireplace carted away, the wood paneling stripped from the walls. The bookshelves remained but stood largely bare, their decorative busts long since removed. The fountain was dry, its marble rim etched with lime. Even the coins in the fountain had been taken!

Most of the staff had been dismissed; only a handful of clerks remained. And they were all gathered now, their faces solemn, their voices hushed with murmured speculation. A heavy stillness hung in the air.

"What are my employees doing, Spirit?" Cratchit asked as he walked unseen among them. "What are they whispering about?"

Peter appeared and stepped to the front of the assembled staff. He looked drawn and exhausted, his clothes rumpled, his eyes bloodshot. Clearing his throat, he began: "It is with great sadness I must inform you that Cratchit and Sons is being sold."

Gasps and murmurs spread through the group.

"The company is being sold? Impossible!" Cratchit protested. "There must be some mistake, Spirit."

Peter's voice wavered as he continued. "In years past, this firm made some unwise business decisions and expenditures—"

A loud metallic clatter erupted from the neglected radiator system—pipes hammering, joints rattling. The echo reverberated throughout the room. Peter paused, waiting for the noise to subside. No one reacted to the interruption; the staff had grown accustomed to it. The clanging ended, as it always did, with a long, hissing release—like a death gasp.

Peter cleared his throat and continued. "I've used my personal savings to keep the company solvent. But now, I'm afraid even that is exhausted. The new ownership takes over tomorrow. I thank you all for your service, and I know that were my father here—he would thank you as well."

Silence fell. The staff bowed their heads, the weight of the moment settling over them. Hobbs finally spoke up. "Sir—who are the new owners?"

Peter did not answer. He simply turned slowly and walked toward his father's office, the staff parting for him like mourners before a coffin.

Inside Cratchit's office, the air was frigid despite a fire burning in the hearth. Seated in front of his father's desk was the man who had orchestrated the company's takeover—Mr. Thatch.

Peter crossed to the chair behind the desk, moving with the stiffness of a man holding himself together by force of will. He sat opposite Thatch, pulled out his pill box, and opened it with unsteady hands.

Empty.

For a moment, panic touched his face. But then another box, this one full, slid across the polished wood. Peter reached for the pills, but Thatch withdrew them quickly.

"First things first," he insisted. With calculated patience, he pushed a stack of documents forward. Despite the cold, sweat beaded on Peter's brow. Reluctantly, he dipped a pen in the inkwell and began to sign.

"You may be interested to know," Thatch said, "that acquiring your firm is the final action I'm taking with my company. I'm retiring."

"How fortunate for you," Peter said dryly. The scratch of the nib against parchment was the only other sound in the room.

"The wealth I've amassed," Thatch continued, "will afford me quite a comfortable life. A pity the same can't be said for Cratchit and Sons."

"I assume you won't be retaining that name for the company," said Peter.

"Regrettably, no," Thatch replied. "I was thinking Marley and Company—in honor of Mr. Scrooge's former business partner. It has a nice symmetry, don't you think—from Scrooge and Marley, now back to Marley and Company?"

"You're handling Jacob Marley's estate?" Peter asked, puzzled.

"There's nothing left of Mr. Marley's estate," Thatch responded. His attention drifted to a cockroach that had climbed up the desk, its antennae twitching. "Did you know that Jacob Marley had two sons?"

"Yes. I believe both now deceased."

Thatch raised an eyebrow. "One was cunning and ruthless. He had his brother committed—to secure their father's inheritance entirely for himself. He squandered it all and died a pauper."

Whack! Thatch's palm came down like a judge's gavel, making Peter jump. Thatch lifted his palm with chilling slowness, revealing the crushed insect, its legs still twitching. He plucked it between two fingers, holding it aloft.

"Delicacies such as this are how most of us survived in the asylum," he said casually. Then, with a flick of his fingers that was almost elegant, he cast the roach into the fire.

Peter's face blanched as the truth dawned on him. He looked up slowly and Thatch's dark, piercing eyes met his own—cold and unblinking.

"You're Jacob Marley's son," Peter said.

"The same," Thatch confirmed.

"You changed your name."

"Not just my name," Thatch said, emphasizing every word. "I—changed—*everything*."

Peter swallowed, eyes fixed on Thatch as if staring at a ghost. "I heard you were dead."

"I was. In a way," Thatch replied. "But I came back."

He snatched the papers with a sudden sweep of his hand and leaned over the desk. His breath was cold against Peter's face.

"Boo."

Peter recoiled, stumbling to his feet and knocking his chair backward in a clatter of wood and metal.

Thatch stood, amused, placing the signed documents in a leather satchel. "A pleasure to do business with you, young Cratchit," he said, pushing the pill box across the desk with one finger. "An early Christmas present."

Peter stared at the box of pills, every nerve straining for relief. He closed his eyes, fighting the anxiety that surged through his body.

When he opened them again—Thatch was gone.

"Why am I absent, Spirit?" Cratchit asked, his voice rising with urgency. "Where will I be in days to come? Show me!"

The Spirit responded by lifting its skeletal arm. A dense fog engulfed the room in whiteness so thick that Cratchit could no longer see the Phantom. Then, as suddenly as it had come, the fog cleared. Cratchit now stood alone among weathered headstones.

A hush hung over the land of the dead, broken only by the stir of wind through the barren trees. He turned slowly in confusion, his breath catching as his eyes landed on the stone before him.

"Scrooge's grave," he whispered.

A crack of lightning split the sky, revealing for a moment the Phantom floating in the distance, its long black garments drifting in the wind like smoke from a pyre.

Cratchit shouted to the apparition. "Spirit, why bring me here? Do you wish to remind me how you changed Ebenezer's heart? Is that the lesson I'm to learn?"

The Phantom gave no answer.

"What's the matter? Say something, blast you!"

The Phantom remained mute.

"Here, let me say it *for* you then!"

With a nervous laugh, Cratchit snapped a small branch from the tree overhead. He broke off a few twigs to shape a crude mimicry of the Spirit's hand—with one long twig for the Spirit's bony finger—hiding his own hand so that the branch now stuck out of his coat sleeve.

"Bob Cratchit, behold your former partner, Ebenezer Scrooge!" he bellowed in a deep voice, pointing at the gravestone dramatically. "A man of honor, unlike you. A man of virtue, unlike you. A man of character, *unlike you*!"

In answer, the Phantom lifted its arm and beckoned him forward.

"Come to you? I think not!" Cratchit said. "I've had enough hocus pocus for one night!"

But the Spirit raised its hand high and Cratchit felt his feet leave the earth, drawn upward as if dangling on unseen strings. With a silent gust, he flew through the air, pulled by invisible forces past trees, headstones, marble benches. With a sudden drop, Cratchit landed at the Phantom's feet.

Breathing heavily, he looked up to see the Spirit pointing again.

Cratchit followed the line of its gesture and saw, cloaked in mist, a solitary woman standing among the graves, her head bowed.

"Belinda?" he gasped. He rose, crossed to her, and stood by her side, wishing that she could feel his presence.

"Belinda. Why are you crying, my dear?"

She gave no reply. Her eyes remained fixed on the headstone before her. Cratchit turned to read the inscription carved into the stone: 'ABIGAIL CRATCHIT, BELOVED WIFE AND MOTHER.'

"Abigail," he whispered, his throat tightening.

Belinda knelt slowly, her shoulders heavy with grief, and laid a small bouquet of flowers at the base of the stone.

"I miss you, Mother," she said, barely above a whisper. "More than you know." She wiped her eyes on her sleeve, then picked up a worn wicker basket. Without another word, she turned and walked away, her figure fading into the gray.

For a moment longer, Cratchit stood staring at the stone that bore his wife's name. Then, with a heavy heart, he turned and followed his daughter's fading silhouette into the night.

Belinda walked alone through the streets of London. The cold clung to the city like a shroud, and though her coat was neatly mended, it offered little protection from the biting air. With her arms crossed tightly over her chest, she moved with quiet purpose. Cratchit and the Spirit followed at a distance, unseen, their steps making no imprint on this world.

She stopped in front of a handsome townhome with windows aglow. A fine brass knocker gleamed on the freshly painted door. Etched into the polished transom were the initials: *R. Y.* Belinda gazed through the frosted glass for a long, motionless moment—then turned and continued down the street.

"Why did she pause, Spirit?" Cratchit asked. "Who lives there?" He stepped forward and looked inside.

A fire crackled in the hearth, casting a golden glow upon the paneled walls and richly appointed furnishings. Randall Yates reclined near the blaze, impeccably dressed in a fitted waistcoat. He was accessorized in gold: pocket watch, matching cufflinks, a wedding band. His shoes, a pair of soft leather mojaris, rested on a silk ottoman.

"That is my clerk. How could he afford such a place?" Cratchit murmured, his hand resting against the window-pane.

Beside Randall was his wife, a woman of striking beauty, her dark hair drawn back with a small jeweled pin. Her rounded belly was a quiet testament to the child they awaited. She hummed softly while making a colorful paper chain for the Christmas tree.

"Tell me Spirit," Cratchit asked, "did Randall send the letter he wrote to his father?"

The Specter did not answer.

Cratchit leaned in closer to the glass and caught sight of a silver-framed wedding portrait upon the mantel: Randall in a tailored morning coat, a silk stole crossing his chest in the Bengali fashion—his bride adorned in a silk sari and delicate maang tikka.

“That’s the man my daughter was to marry,” Cratchit remarked sadly, “were it not for me.”

His shoulders tensed, his jaw tightened, and his hand curled into a fist.

“Were it not for me!” he cried out, the regret unbearable.

He struck his chest with a sharp blow. Again. And again. And again.

As if hurting himself might make the pain go away.

Self-loathing surged within him. He wished he could vanish into the fog. To feel nothing. To become nothing.

He turned to the Phantom, hoping for a flicker of compassion. But the Spirit offered none. Its skeletal arm lifted once more, pointing forward with unyielding finality. Cratchit steadied his breath and followed, quickening his pace, for Belinda was already drifting from view.

Soon, a hospital loomed before them, cold and drab under the weight of night. Belinda mounted the stone steps slowly, her basket growing heavy in her arms. Cratchit and the Ghost followed.

Inside, the corridors were lined with rows of iron-framed beds, each occupied by patients wrapped in woolen blankets and faded linens. Groans and murmurs echoed faintly off tiled walls. The air was heavy with the smell of antiseptic and bleach. Belinda passed bed after bed until she came to one near the far end.

There, propped up against a thin pillow, lay her father. Cratchit froze, breath catching in his throat when he saw the withered shell of a man he was to become—his head bandaged, his skin pale and waxen. Dark circles etched themselves beneath dull, lifeless eyes. He stared straight ahead, unseeing.

Belinda leaned down and pressed her lips gently to his forehead. "Merry Christmas, Father," she whispered. She sat beside him and began unpacking her basket. From the neighboring bed, a feisty elderly matron leaned over the gap between them.

"Just stares off into space all day, he does," said Miss Priddy. "Lord knows where his mind is at."

Belinda smiled at her politely, then turned to her father. "I brought something special for you today. A plum pudding. Just as Mother made it every Christmas."

Bob had no reaction, not even a blink.

Miss Priddy leaned closer. "He ain't much for conversation, is he? I talk to him all the time, but he's never said a word back. I hear he nearly had his skull crushed by a horse's hoof. Stumbled out of a pub and walked straight into the path of a hansom, they say. Almost kilt him."

Belinda didn't reply. Miss Priddy dropped her voice to a conspiring whisper. "By the by, next time you come, deary, might you see your way clear to bring me a spot of whiskey?"

Belinda glanced at her sideways. "It's purely for medicinal purposes, I can assure you, my dear," Miss Priddy added.

From a few beds down, an older man with heavy brows, Mr. Crumley, joined in the conversation. "'Ere now, Miss Priddy. The young lady came to see her father, not to entertain an old maid like yourself. Leave her be."

"A pint would do nicely, my dear," Miss Priddy went on as though she hadn't heard.

“You’re daft, you are,” Mr. Crumley chuckled. “You should be institutionalized for your own good.”

“A very nice sentiment to express at Christmas time, Mr. Crumley,” she admonished him.

“Insanity knows no season, Miss Priddy. A mind like yours is just as loony in December as it is in June.”

Cratchit looked down at the vacant expression of his future self. Just moments ago, outside Randall’s home, he had wished to feel nothing. Now, he saw before him that wish fulfilled.

“Is this what I am to become, Spirit?” he cried. “A man, but not really a man at all? Helpless. Unfeeling. Oblivious. No. No, I would rather be dead!” He turned to Belinda. “Go!” he shouted. “Run away from this place as fast as you can, and never come back! I don’t want to live! Not like this. *Not like this!*”

Cratchit sank to his knees, overcome, breath catching in his throat. The lamplight cast a gentle halo over Belinda’s still form. He reached for her hand, but all he touched was air. A broken sound escaped him—half gasp, half prayer.

“Forgive me, Belinda,” he sobbed. “Forgive me, my precious daughter.”

Slowly, with every joint resisting, he stood, the weight of sorrow hanging from his frame. Turning to the Spirit, overcome with remorse, he spoke in a hoarse whisper: “Show me no more.”

The Phantom raised its arm, then slowly lowered it. The world twisted once more.

Standing in the narrow hallway of a decaying tenement, Cratchit winced at the squalor; plaster walls pocketed with holes, streaked with the residue of old leaks. The ceiling wept steadily into a rusted bucket. Splintered floorboards, warped and studded with nail heads, lay slick with grime. A rat darted across the corridor and vanished into a hole in the baseboard.

And yet, wafting through the filth and rot, there came music—pure, mournful, transcendent. A solo violin played Schubert's *Serenade No. 4*, each note haunting as a lament, incongruously beautiful amid the ruin.

Cratchit shivered, his voice hushed with unease. "What's here, Spirit? Who lives in this wretched place?"

The Spirit moved forward and passed through the wall. Cratchit, with mounting dread, followed.

They entered a dim, windowed flat lit only by the dying glow of a streetlamp beyond a grime-frosted pane. A lone figure stood near the window, bow in hand, coaxing sorrow from the strings.

"Tim!" Cratchit gasped, his hand reaching out instinctively.

He hurried forward, coming to stand beside the gaunt, disheveled form of his son. Tim's wrinkled clothes hung from him loosely. Empty liquor bottles cluttered the floor, and the stench of old spirits mingled with the acrid smell of spoiled food and mold.

Tim played the final notes of the *Serenade* with aching precision, then paused for a moment before gently placing his violin and bow in a battered case.

Cratchit turned desperately to the Spirit. "Is this what is to become of my family? Even Tim?"

His son stood still, staring out at London as snow blanketed the rooftops in oppressive silence.

Cratchit looked at him, heartbroken, his voice catching. "I loved him as much as any father could love a son. What have I done?"

Suddenly, with a sharp motion that startled Cratchit, Tim grabbed the heavy drapes and yanked them down, sending dust swirling through the stale air. He deftly detached the drapery cord and held it up, pulling it taut to test its strength.

With mechanical precision, he dragged a wooden chair to the center of the room and tossed the cord over a ceiling beam. Cratchit recoiled, his eyes wide with horror.

"No," he whispered, breathless.

Tim's hands moved with terrifying calm as he wound the cord into a noose.

"No. No, Spirit!" Cratchit cried, his voice rising with panic. "This must be stopped! Help me! You must help me, I beg you!" He lunged for the drapery cord, but his hands passed through the rope.

"Spirit, this must not happen," he pleaded, his voice cracking. "Punish me for the mistakes I've made in my life, but do not punish my son!"

The noose hung ready. Tim stepped onto the chair.

"Tim! I promise, whatever pain you feel, I will take it away! For God's sake, don't do this!"

Frantic, Cratchit sank to his knees and reached for the chair, trying to pull it away. But again, his arms grasped only air.

"Good Spirit, answer me, I pray you!" he begged the Phantom, tears streaming down his face. "Are these visions of what will happen, or can these shadows be changed if I change my life?" His voice caught in his throat, but he forced himself to continue. "Just as Ebenezer was given a second chance, grant me a reprieve and I will show you I can again become the man I once was. I will not forget these lessons! I will keep Christmas in my heart all the year long!"

He reached for the Spirit, clutching its garment. "Pity me, I beg you! Have mercy!" he sobbed. Cratchit lowered his head and closed his eyes, unable to contain his anguish. "Have mercy. Have mercy. Have mercy—"

When he opened his eyes again, he was clinging to the sleeve of his overcoat, which he had draped over a chair the night before.

He blinked. The chill of the tenement was gone. The mysterious Phantom had vanished. He let go of the coat sleeve and stood, cautiously, in the quiet familiarity of his offices.

He glanced about, scarcely daring to believe. "I'm back," he whispered. "It's over!"

Disbelief gave way to wild elation. "I've been given a second chance!" he cried, flinging his arms wide. He laughed aloud, giddy with gratitude.

But the laughter died in his throat.

A long, misshapen shadow appeared on the floor in front of him, growing with unnatural speed. Behind him came the sound of labored breathing, low and guttural, as if from some monstrous thing barely able to contain its hunger.

He turned slowly, looked up, and gasped.

Standing over him was a grotesque beast, its eyes sunken deep into its skull, its mouth stretched in a permanent grin of jagged teeth.

Stave Five

Christmas Day

Cratchit bolted upright in his chair, screaming. His breath came in halted gasps, his eyes darting left and right. He peered behind the chair, then turned back quickly. Was he awake—or was this still a dream?

If it was a dream, he wanted no more of it! He slapped one cheek, then the other. His eyes landed on the punchbowl, still half-full from last night's party. Cratchit raced over and plunged his face into the bowl. Jerking upright, dripping and sputtering, he looked around again, surveying the room. No beasts. No phantoms. He let out a long sigh of relief.

He caught sight of the destroyed grandfather clock—the very one he'd shot the night before. A grin curled across his face.

"Killing time!" he laughed, recalling the Spirit's awful pun. "Who would have guessed ghosts had such a marvelous sense of humor?" Raising his arms, he shouted to the ether above. "Thank you, spirits! I shall be forever in your debt!"

As he put on his coat, he paused to reflect, praying that it was not too late to save his family. His eyes fell upon the scarf his wife had made for him hanging from his coat pocket.

"Can all the terrible things I've done truly be undone?" he wondered.

Cratchit pulled the scarf from his pocket, holding it gently in his hands before wrapping it around his neck and grabbing his hat.

There was no time to lose. He dashed out the door.

Cratchit emerged from the building as though from a tomb, blinking at the morning light. His limbs were stiff with cold, but his stride lengthened with every step, urgency mounting in his chest.

As he ran through the town square, children darted past him, trailed by ribbons and laughter. A snowball exploded against his backside. Cratchit turned, grinning, and called out, "Merry Christmas, my fine young fellow!" Then to an old woman pushing a cart of roasted chestnuts: "And to you, madam! A Merry Christmas!" Passing the statue of Scrooge, he tipped his hat. "Merry Christmas, Ebenezer!"

He felt younger than he had in years. At the top of his street, he saw boys racing down the frozen slide. Without breaking stride, Cratchit charged onto the ice, his leather soles skimming across it as the boys cheered. He bounded off the end and kept running, laughing aloud.

Past terraced houses he flew until, at last, he reached his own. Taking the steps two at a time, he threw open the door.

In the parlor, Belinda stood before the mirror, fastening her coat. "Merry Christmas, my dear!" Cratchit said gaily, breathless with excitement.

She turned without smiling. "I waited up for you last night. You never came home."

"It will never happen again, I promise you," he said, voice soft and earnest.

"I promise you," she repeated, rolling her eyes. "How easily those words roll off your lips. They've become very familiar to me. And completely meaningless."

She picked up her purse and stepped past him. "Your breakfast is on the stove," she added, hand on the door. "I'm going to Christmas services."

"May I join you?"

She hesitated, her hand still on the knob. Then, slowly, she turned to face him.

"I'll only be a moment," he said. "Would you wait for me, Belinda?"

Her expression softened. She searched his face—his kind eyes, his genuine smile, his quiet humility. There, in the lines and shadows, she glimpsed the father she once knew. She studied him for a moment longer, then gave a small, astonished nod.

He stepped closer. "How I've crushed your spirit, my child. How blind I've been all these years. If only I could take away the suffering I've caused you."

His fingers brushed her sleeves, resting where scars lay hidden. "Can you ever forgive a foolish old man for being so blind?"

"I forgive you, Father," she said quietly, the change in him still difficult to grasp.

"Randall is a fortunate man indeed," he said, smiling. "Nothing would please me more than for him to ask for your hand in marriage."

Her eyes widened. She pressed her hands to her mouth as tears welled. Throwing her arms around her father, she hugged him tightly. Then, pulling back just slightly, she asked, "But do you really suppose that he might propose one day?"

Cratchit smiled and rested his hand gently on her cheek. "Let's just say—it's something I've dreamt of."

Emotion swelled in her chest as she embraced him once more, holding tight.

"There is one thing I ask you to do for me," he said. "After services, go to your mother. If she allows it, I should like to call on her today and beg her forgiveness. Tell her—tell her that this house is not a *home* without her."

Belinda's smile broadened. For the first time in a long while, she believed the words he spoke. "I'll tell her," she said.

A joyous yap came from the next room. Chester bounded around the corner and leapt into Cratchit's arms. The little dog licked his master's face with gleeful abandon. Cratchit laughed, then lifted his eyes to the ceiling. "Tim. Is he in his room?" he asked Belinda.

Tim lay sprawled across his bed, still dressed from the day before, his clothes wrinkled and stained. His breath came slow and heavy. The room reeked of spirits and sweat. A half-empty bottle of rum rested on the nightstand.

Cratchit entered quietly and stood beside the bed, gazing down at his son. A wave of memories washed over him. He closed his eyes and could see Tim as a frail child, riding on his shoulders. He galloped and neighed like a horse as Tim laughed above, tiny arms wrapped around his neck.

"I was a father to you once, Tim," he whispered. "A good father. As God is my witness, I will be again. I swear it."

In the parlor below, Belinda waited for her father on the sofa. From the corner of her eye, she caught a glimpse of something falling past the picture window. A moment later, another object—smaller, shinier—fell in its wake. Curious, she rose and stepped to the window.

In the small garden, among the flowers, lay a rum bottle with its contents seeping into the soil. Beside it rested her father's silver flask.

Four days later, Cratchit sat alone at his desk, melting a stick of red wax over a candle flame. Though it was a business day, the offices were silent. He had granted the staff the week off. No one had returned since the Christmas party, and he himself had not stepped inside since departing the building on Christmas morning.

He turned the wax slowly in the flame, watching it soften. This was the day he had silently braced for. Mr. Thatch had called a meeting to disclose the results of Revaluation Day. Cratchit knew the news would not be kind. Though Thatch spoke with the smooth assurance of a friend, the Ghosts had revealed the truth. His scheme was not to assist the firm, but to crush it. It was a calculated betrayal, meant to leave him destitute—and place the business in the hands of men who had never earned it.

His hand trembled slightly as he moved the wax stick from the candle flame to just above an envelope, allowing a few drops to fall onto the flap. He pressed a small brass stamp into the warm wax to seal it.

He turned the envelope over in his hand. It was addressed to his youngest daughter Jenny, in America.

Peter appeared at the doorway. "They're here, Father."

Cratchit nodded and drew a deep breath, setting the letter aside. Moments later, Thatch entered, followed by Hawkins, Quill, and Ramsey. Cratchit gestured toward the chairs, and they all sat, save Thatch and Peter. Thatch removed his hat and placed it on the desk beside the hourglass he had gifted Cratchit on Christmas Eve.

"Gentlemen," Thatch said, "I trust that we find you both in good spirits."

"We are," Cratchit replied. "And we trust you bring news that will *keep* us in good spirits."

"Yes, well—" Thatch began, but stopped when he saw Mary standing in the office doorway.

"I hope you don't mind, gentlemen," said Cratchit. "I've invited Miss Fielding to join us today and take notes, for the sake of accuracy."

Thatch, though visibly irritated, mustered a brittle smile. "Not at all. Good day," he said with stiff civility.

"Good day, Miss—?" Mary prompted.

Thatch's jaw tightened. "Miss *Fielding*," he said, as though the name itself left a sour taste.

Mary nodded to Thatch, then to the others, and crossed the room with quiet confidence. She seated herself beside Cratchit's desk and opened her notebook, pen poised.

"Before we begin," Cratchit said, "I have a confession to make."

He rose from his chair and paused, folding his hands.

"As you know, Mr. Scrooge was released from his position due to grievous errors in his ledgers. But he was not to blame. *His* mind was sharp, *mine* was corrupted. Those errors were purposely put there—*by me*."

Mary let out an involuntary gasp. Peter's face stiffened.

"You ask why," Cratchit continued. "I'll tell you: Vanity. Pride. I imagined myself more important than I was. In doing so, I failed my family. I betrayed my friend. And I believe I very nearly sold my soul."

Thatch raised a brow. Cratchit's eyes moved to the flickering candle flame.

"But by the grace of God, I've been given a second chance. My family is again my priority, as they should always have been. The man I strive to be *now*—is the man I once *was*."

He looked around the room. Peter remained stoic. Mary blinked back tears. The four businessmen were uninterested, eager to proceed.

As Cratchit sat back down, Thatch patronized him with a dismissive, "Well said, old fellow." He nodded to Hawkins, who produced a set of documents for Cratchit and Peter.

"I do wish we were meeting under more cheerful circumstances, Bob," he said. "As you know, you have three loans outstanding with us. As was their privilege, the Board of Directors imposed a rate increase on each one, effective Christmas Day. The increase was—substantial."

"Substantial?" Peter repeated, scanning the numbers. "There are far better words to describe these increases. Unscrupulous. Unwarranted. Unethical."

"Devastating," said Cratchit, his eyes fixed on the page. "How is this possible? You assured me—"

Thatch raised his hands slightly, as if lamenting the outcome. "I argued for favorable terms, of course. I did all I could, truly, but I was overruled by the Board. It's nothing personal. Merely business."

"Business," Cratchit echoed. "Are you trying to *ruin* my business?"

There was a pause before Thatch answered. "Of course not, Bob. We're your friends."

Cratchit looked from Thatch to the three stone-faced businessmen. How could he have been so blind all these years, failing to see their selfish, soulless natures?

His gaze dropped to the hourglass. The final grains of sand drifted downward—slowly, inevitably—until the upper chamber was drained and spent.

Like an empty chalice.

Cratchit leaned forward, holding his head in his hands as he stared at the documents. Mary reached over and placed her hand on his arm.

The businessmen exchanged knowing glances, bracing for the familiar sequence: shock, rage, pleading—then despair. They had brokered the collapse of enough firms to recognize the pattern. Witnessing such anguish had become routine. Tedious, even.

But Cratchit sat in silence, not uttering a word.

"Well," Thatch said finally, as the men started to rise. "We'll leave you to—"

"Peter," Cratchit interrupted, turning to his son. "I believe you have something to say?"

Peter nodded, cleared his throat, and addressed the men. "We'd like to break the contracts."

The businessmen paused for a moment, taken aback, then started chuckling heartily amongst themselves. Even Thatch couldn't resist a snicker.

"As I was saying," Peter continued, "we are exercising our right to repudiate these agreements due to their—"

"Stop." Thatch cut him off with the lift of his hand. "You can't do that."

"We can and we are," Peter said.

Thatch sighed heavily. "Honestly, I expected a better grasp of the law from you, young Cratchit. You should know that the *only* way the contracts can be repudiated is if they have been violated in some way. Which they haven't."

"Oh, but they have, Mr. Marley—" Cratchit said.

There was a beat of silence.

"—I mean, Mr. Thatch."

He searched for a reaction from Thatch, but all he detected was a slight twitch of his lips. The three business partners looked at each other, a flicker of discomfort passed between them.

Thatch smiled. "It seems our friends have uncovered a piece of my past that I've tried to keep buried. Bravo, well done. However, the fact that I changed my name many years ago has no bearing on our business arrangements."

"Oh, but it does," Peter insisted. "When you were in—hospital—you lost the right to act legally in your own name."

"True," Thatch conceded. "However, I regained that right when I received a certificate of recovery upon my release."

"I expected a better grasp of the law from you, Mr. Thatch," Peter countered. "Once declared incompetent, a man must file a petition with the Court of Chancery to restore his legal status."

"You never filed a petition," Cratchit added, rising to his feet, "which means—on paper—you don't exist."

Thatch blinked, nothing more.

Peter concluded, "The contracts were signed by someone without any legal authority. And that is why—we can break them."

"This is madness!" Hawkins cried. The room erupted into a storm of raised voices—threats, accusations, disbelief. Thatch calmly raised his hand, quieting the others.

"Bob," he said, turning to Cratchit, "tell us you're not allowing this."

"Not only am I allowing it," Cratchit replied, stepping in front of his desk. "I'm *insisting* on it." He turned to Mary. "That was quite well said. Did you write that down, Miss Fielding?"

"Every word, Mr. Cratchit," she replied.

"All contracts Mr. Thatch signed for the firm during his tenure," Peter resumed, "are now open to challenge. News such as this will no doubt have adverse effects on *your* company, gentlemen. Which is why we arranged this morning to sell short a substantial number of your shares. Should things go as poorly for you as we expect, *we* will soon become your majority shareholders."

The room erupted in outbursts again.

"We took you into our confidence, Cratchit!" one businessman said.

"We've been beyond generous with you," another added.

"Is this how you treat *friends*?" the other demanded.

"No," Cratchit replied. "It's how I treat *thieves.*"

Their shocked expressions bore not the mark of injured honor, but of rogues suddenly unmasked in full daylight.

Cratchit glanced again at Mary. "I believe we're finished with notes, Miss Fielding. Was there anything *you* wished to add?"

Mary gently closed her notebook and replied, "There is," before rising to her feet. "First, I'd like to say—" She turned to Cratchit and Peter, her eyes bright with admiration. "Hell's bells, that was impressive! Well done, gentlemen."

A collective murmur of disapproval stirred among the businessmen, who found her turn of phrase unladylike and unbecoming, while the Cratchit men struggled to suppress their grins.

Mary then faced the four financiers, her expression hardening. "As for you gentlemen—there's an old Yiddish saying that comes to mind, and I wish it for you with all my heart: *A kholerye zolstu krign.* Especially *you,* Mr. Thatch."

She took a few deliberate steps forward and stopped squarely before him. His world, she knew, was unravelling. In Thatch's face, she saw something unusual. A look she had never seen before: *Uncertainty.* The sight of it made her smile.

"A shekel for your thoughts," she said with a softness that belied the blow.

With that, she turned and departed, chin high and notebook clutched to her chest.

"That concludes our business, gentlemen," Peter said. "Good day." He moved forward to show them the door, but Thatch put his arm out, stopping him.

"I'll go back to the Board," he said to Cratchit, an urgency in his voice now. "I will *demand* that they give you favorable terms. No interest for the next three years. No, I'll insist on five. They'll listen to me!"

Cratchit stood silent, giving no reply.

His mind racing, Thatch's face suddenly brightened.

"*A ring!*" he exclaimed. "You shall have your ring! I have connections—men who owe me favors. I'll see that the proper palms are greased. You'll be one of us in no time. How does *that* sound?"

Cratchit looked at Thatch's ring, its silver chalice now worn and tarnished.

"It sounds like the ramblings of a desperate man," Cratchit replied. He picked up Thatch's hat from the desk.

Thatch forced a smile, placing his hand on Cratchit's shoulder. "Bob, I beg you to reconsider—"

"It's done, Marley," Cratchit said, holding out the hat. *"It's over."*

Thatch's smile disappeared. He looked down at his hat, then back at Cratchit. With the speed of a serpent's strike, Thatch's hand went from Cratchit's shoulder to his throat, squeezing tightly.

Peter quickly moved to intervene, but the three men grabbed his arms, restraining him.

"Do you think you've won?" Thatch sneered. "This is an inconvenience, nothing more. But you, Bob Cratchit—you will be reviled among men."

Cratchit wrenched himself free of Thatch's grip, gasping for air as he staggered backwards toward the door. His eyes darted around the room, searching for anything he could use as a weapon.

And there it was—his cane—propped against the desk just behind Thatch.

Thatch followed Cratchit's gaze to the cane. A thin, knowing smile crept across his face. Without breaking eye contact, he reached back and took it for himself.

"Looking for this, my friend?" he said, lifting the cane with mock civility.

Suddenly, with a savage swing, he struck the desk lamp. The glass exploded. Shards flew and lamp oil spilled onto the floorboards.

"I will see to it that your reputation is destroyed," Thatch spat, advancing on him. "You will curse the day you ever met us!"

"I already do," Cratchit said, trying to keep distance between them.

But Thatch lunged and struck him in the side with the cane. Cratchit winced and lurched toward his desk.

Thatch raged on: "The Cratchit name will be disgraced. You will beg your family for forgiveness!"

"I already have," came the reply.

Thatch raised the cane again and swung it like a club, striking Cratchit across the temple.

Peter struggled to break free, but the three men held him fast.

Cratchit stumbled, blood dripping from his mouth, yet stayed upright, defiant. As he placed a hand on the desk to steady himself, his fingers brushed against something cold to the touch.

"You will search that dull-witted brain of yours for answers, but there will be none!" Thatch seethed, closing in on his prey once again. "Because you are a simpleton. A commoner. You will never be a Knight Paragon. Never! You will—"

The last words never came. Cratchit swung the heavy pewter hourglass straight into Thatch's jaw. Glass shattered, and a burst of sand poured across the floor.

Cratchit straightened, wiping the blood from his lip.

"Life's too short for long speeches," he said.

Injured, but shaking off the blow, Thatch touched the deep gash on his face, feeling the warm blood on his fingers. With the fury of a wounded beast, he lunged at Cratchit.

The hourglass slipped from Cratchit's grasp as the two men crashed into the desk. The lit candle toppled, rolled off the edge, and dropped into the splattered lamp oil. Flames leapt up instantly.

Thatch had Cratchit pinned against the table. Their eyes fell on the paperknife resting beside the inkstand. Both reached for it—Cratchit a heartbeat too slow.

Thatch seized the knife and slashed, the blade catching Cratchit's forearm. He looked down as blood soaked into his white shirt sleeve. Thatch thrust, but Cratchit caught his wrist. He pushed back with all his strength, attempting to keep the blade from his throat, but Thatch was stronger.

"You would do well to die like a man," he advised.

"I would much prefer to *live* like one," Cratchit said.

Thatch's lips curled into a grin. "That's no longer an option," he whispered.

With a burst of rage, Thatch broke free of Cratchit's grip and let out a demonic growl. Flames from the spreading fire leapt higher as he raised the knife to strike a lethal blow.

Crack! A thunderous shot split the air. For the span of a breath, the room froze.

Thatch's hand opened, releasing the knife. It clattered to the floor.

He turned to Cratchit, his face contorted with surprise and pain. Cratchit looked into his eyes and felt a flash of pity for the man.

But then he watched, confused and horrified, as the same hand came down, clamping tightly around his throat.

For one second. Two. Three.

As Cratchit's face reddened, Thatch's turned deathly pale. His grip weakened, life draining from his body. At last, he released his hold and collapsed, motionless, across the desk.

All eyes turned to the man standing inside the doorway.

It was the soldier.

In his hand was the flintlock pistol—the one Cratchit had fired on Christmas morning. A wisp of smoke curled from the pistol's barrel, mingling with the haze already billowing from the burning lamp oil. Peter broke free from the stunned businessmen, tore off his coat, and began beating at the flames.

The soldier motioned with the gun for Hawkings, Quill, and Ramsey to leave. They gladly obliged him, filing out of the office as fast as their feet allowed.

Peter extinguished the flames in short order. With the floor still smoldering, he hurried to his father's side. Grabbing a scarf from the hat rack, he wrapped it tightly around Cratchit's arm wound.

"Sorry if I—interrupted your meeting," the soldier said dryly. "I heard shouting. And the gun was lying there on a table."

From outside the window, the muffled strains of passing carolers singing *God Rest Ye Merry Gentlemen* could be heard. The men looked over at Thatch, who lay across the desk, dead as a door-nail. The song was a strange benediction for a gentleman who, at the moment, did not seem in the least bit merry, but was in fact, at rest.

The soldier stepped forward, broken glass crunching softly under his boots. He placed the pistol on the desk next to Thatch. "I'll notify the constable," he said, starting to walk out of the room. Cratchit stopped him.

"Thank you, Mister—"

"Leeds, sir," the soldier said. "Ben Leeds."

"Ben," Cratchit repeated. The name triggered a memory. His eyes grew wide.

"Benjamin."

The mystic Katura said his destiny would be changed by a man named Benjamin.

Leeds nodded to Cratchit. "At your service, sir." He also gave a brief nod to Peter before stepping out of the room.

The office was deathly still. The choir outside had moved on, and the only sound was the quiet ticking of a pocket watch.

His face scratched and bloodied, Cratchit surveyed the room.

"I've made a mess of things, haven't I?" he asked with a deep sigh.

Peter did not hesitate. "Yes, you have." Then after a brief pause, he added, "And thank God for it."

A smile slowly broke across Peter's face, broad and sincere.

"I'm proud of you, Father," he said. "Well played."

He embraced Cratchit, who for a moment remained stock-still, not expecting Peter's rare show of affection. Slowly, joyfully, he returned the embrace, wrapping his arms around his son.

"Things will be different now, Peter," Cratchit whispered. "I promise you. You'll see. You'll see."

And indeed, things were different. Under Peter Cratchit's steady hand, the company—once teetering on the brink—was being quietly rehabilitated, thanks in large part to a fresh flow of income from Thatch's company, which they now controlled.

Cratchit found comfort in the revival of his business, but it was the restoration of his family that brought true gladness to his heart. For in the pews of their church one Christmas morning, framed in the jewel-toned glow of stained glass and the solemn cadence of a hymn, his family stood whole once more.

Peter held his wife's hand as she cradled their newborn daughter.

Martha sang sweetly beside Thomas, who was oblivious to his nephew's mischievous prank: placing a tack on the pew where his uncle was about to sit.

Belinda stood beside Randall, her hand resting lightly on his arm, while the wedding band on her finger caught the light and scattered it in a quiet shimmer.

Miles away, Tim and Mary walked hand in hand along the Cliffs of Moher overlooking the restless sea. Near them, smoke curled from the chimney of a small stone cottage cradled in a field of clover that stretched for as far as the eye could see.

As they strolled through the town square, Cratchit looked down lovingly at his wife. She looped her hand through the crook of his arm, her eyes lifting to him with a warmth that held no trace of bitterness. She was simply grateful—to be home again, and to have the man she married return to her.

The bell's clang from the clock tower was no longer ominous or foreboding. Cratchit welcomed it now as a reminder that though time stops for no one, we should pause—regardless of our station in life—to count our blessings. To love our families. To forgive others, and perhaps, to forgive ourselves.

As was now his custom anytime he walked through the square, Cratchit bought a pink carnation from the flower girl who sold them on the corner. She charged a halfpenny, but he always gave her a guinea.

He would place the flower gently at the foot of Scrooge's statue, among the other offerings and tributes the townspeople still brought. Then, as always, he'd give a wink and a nod up to Ebenezer. And Cratchit liked to imagine that, from some quiet corner of heaven, Ebenezer returned it in kind.

Like Scrooge, Bob Cratchit became as good a friend as the good old town of London ever knew. He took the lessons taught by the Spirits to heart, remembering that each day upon this earth was a gift not to be squandered.

He rediscovered the Spirit of Christmas, keeping it better than any man alive.

And so, may the Spirit of Christmas touch us all.

As Tim Cratchit himself would say—God bless us, every one!

Printed in Dunstable, United Kingdom

75579880R00088